It was a damp Thursday night in early March. Luke Green's heart beat faster and faster – and not just because he'd fibbed to his mum to get out of the house.

He'd said he was going over to his mate Frederick Dulac's. Why? So that they could revise together for a German test at school tomorrow morning. But tonight German was the last thing on Luke and Frederick's minds. Instead they would be doing all their talking with their feet. They would be speaking in the world's best and most beautiful language of all: pure football!

Luke rode his bike to the top of Cranham Hill then turned right towards Ash Acre stadium – the home of his beloved local club, Castle Albion FC. It was like diving into a human river. Hordes of fans in blue and white hoops were streaming towards the ground on both pavements and all the way across the road. Then the first dazzling floodlights reared into view on their pylons.

Pedalling slower, Luke gazed up in wonder. It didn't matter how many times he saw these lights, they always gave him a great big buzz. The night air was filled with the stink of burgers and onions. Lovely! Absolutely *gorgeous*. His mum, however, loathed it all as passionately as he loved it. That's why he'd had to lie about where he was going. If she'd known he would be spending the evening under those lights and amid that stink, she would have grounded him for a year. But for Luke, nothing could beat the atmosphere of match night at rickety old Ash Acre. And this wasn't going to be just any match, either.

For tonight – amazingly – it was European night. Under these brilliant but rather elderly floodlights, Castle Albion would be playing Spartak Moscow from Russia in the first leg of the UEFA Cup quarter-final!

Luke knew he wasn't the only person who had to keep pinching himself about this.

"We're Gonna Win The Cup!"
four schoolkids, older than himself, in CAFC scarves and hats sang out. But there was an edge of disbelief in their voices.

"We're Gonna Murder Moscow!"
bellowed another gang of fans as they queued, clutching their precious tickets, to get into the South Side terrace where the ancient rusting roof always looked as if it was about to cave in.

WE'RE ON OUR WAY TO RUSSIA!

Haydn Middleton

▲ SCHOLASTIC

Scholastic Children's Books,
Commonwealth House, 1-19 New Oxford Street,
London, WC1A 1NU, UK
a division of Scholastic Ltd
London ~ New York ~ Toronto ~ Sydney ~ Auckland
Mexico City ~ New Delhi ~ Hong Kong

First published in the UK by Scholastic Ltd, 2000

Text copyright © Haydn Middleton, 2000

ISBN 0 439 99508 6

Typeset by TW Typesetting, Midsomer Norton, Somerset
Printed by The Bath Press, Bath

1 2 3 4 5 6 7 8 9 10

Luke saw a dazed look on their painted faces too.

Albion? In such top-flight European company? It really did stretch the imagination. For this dozy little club, managed by Benny Webb, currently lay twenty-first in Nationwide League Division Three – and, as everybody knows, the league table never lies. Only Hull, Chester and Shrewsbury were keeping Albion off the bottom. And the league season before this one had been even more disastrous: they'd avoided the drop to the Football Conference by a single place.

Yet, in that same season, they also put together the most astonishing FA Cup run of all time. It ended when they *won* the trophy at Wembley – by beating Manchester United. That put them in the hat for this season's UEFA Cup. Incredible, or what?

Then they squeezed past Sliema Wanderers of Malta and Fenerbahce of Turkey before coming up against *über*-team Bayern Munich. Now that really *was* a German test! The stiffest sort possible. But after losing nil-one at home, Albion's bunch of giant-killers rose up and slew the mighty Munichers on their own home turf to win the tie. All of which left them and their fans right here: in the last eight of the competition, facing the finest team in the whole of Russia!

When the crowds grew too dense for Luke to

keep riding, he got off his bike and wheeled it the rest of the way through the multitude. Then he bent down to lock it to the gate of the players' and officials' car park.

"D'you think we're gonna do it tonight, Daddy?" he overheard a kid of eight chirp at his father as they queued at a turnstile. "Have Albion really got a chance?"

"You never can tell with our lot," his dad replied. "Personally I'd be a lot happier if we had the Dog, our super-striker from Armenia, playing. It's such a shame he's unavailable. But one thing's for sure: if we've got young Luke Green on the teamsheet, we've *always* got a chance. Isn't that right, Luke?"

Luke straightened up and grinned at the man. He was surprised to have got this far before anyone recognized him. Usually he was mobbed from at least the top of Cranham Hill. Yet tonight the Albion faithful had been so focused on the massive game ahead, they simply hadn't spotted him.

But now that he'd been pointed out, a huge flock of well-wishers formed around him – firing questions, wanting autographs, touching him to see if he was real. For Luke Green wasn't here just to *watch* Albion versus Spartak. In less than an hour he was going to be out there on the park – the Studless Sensation in his trademark trainers: the home team's creative midfield genius!

"You gonna score tonight, Luke?"

"Any chance of the Dog making an appearance, Studless?"

"What's Benny Webb's game-plan, Luke? Or hasn't he got one as usual?!"

Luke just smiled and shrugged as he scribbled signature after signature, edging his way closer to the players' entrance. Then a soft purr near to his ear made him grin even wider: "Guten Abend, Herr Green. Bist du fertig?"

German. Now Luke wasn't much good at German, but he thought he knew what those words meant: *Good evening, Mr Green. Are you up for it?* He turned and high-fived the young guy who had just said them – his schoolmate, "Cool" Frederick Dulac, who also happened to be Albion's ultra-stylish sweeper.

"Ja," Luke replied, to the surprise of the watching fans. "Ich bin fertig." Which – he hoped – meant *Yes, I'm up for it*. (So they did do *some* German revision, after all.)

"For real," said Cool F, gently tugging Luke free from his worshippers and easing him through the players' entrance. "So let's go rock those Russkies!"

When Luke and Frederick appeared in the dressing room, manager Benny Webb was so relieved he almost fainted. Most people would have fainted already inside that great sheepskin coat of his when all the radiators were blasting away. The big bearded Bossman really did look uneasy, though.

To be fair, he had a lot to look uneasy about as this vital fixture loomed. For one thing, he definitely couldn't call on the services of Dogan "the Dog" Mezir – the club's record foreign signing who was now back in Armenia dealing with "a family problem". For another, he could never be sure that all his *other* players were going to show up in time for the kick-off.

Benny turned and crossed off the boys' names on the big blackboard. "OK that's seven down," he sighed with a weary shake of the head. "Four to go."

"Relax, Benny," club physio, Terry Vaudeville, chirped back. "Everyone's gonna show up tonight

– you can bet your life on it. I told 'em all after training yesterday: you get yourselves 'ere on time ... *or else!*"

"Or else what?" laughed veteran skipper Stuart "Gaffer" Mann as he finished tying up his right bootlace super-tight.

Terry twisted his face into a sadistic grin and rubbed his hands together. "Or else I'll make 'em sit through the video of us against Peterborough!"

"Ooooh!" chorused half a dozen of the others. "That's *cruel!*"

Back in January, when neither Luke nor Frederick had been available, Albion had gone down one-five at home to the Posh. It hadn't been a pretty sight. But results like that *did* tend to happen when the club's two youngest stars weren't playing.

"So who's in the Russkies' line-up tonight then, Boss?" asked central midfielder Narris Phiz, a one-time Trinidad international. "Any surprises, are there?" He winked at striker Carl Davey, who was pulling a large juicy pineapple out of a green Marks and Spencer's bag. Carl smiled and winked back.

"Well – er – yes, I have *seen* their teamsheet," said Benny, looking flustered. "And – um – no. No – I wouldn't say there's any major surprises..."

Carl and Narris grinned at each other. So did the young striker Keats Aberdeen and one of the subs, Casper Franks. They'd been giggling away all week at Benny's efforts to pronounce their Russian opponents' names. More often than not he called the whole team Spar*track*. And as for goalie Filimonov or outfielders Parfyonov, Khlestov, Ketchinov or Tikhonov, he just couldn't get his tongue around them at all. Now it so happened that midfield battler Michael "Half-Fat" Milkes had Russian grand-parents, and he'd done his best to help Benny out. "Just remember," he kept on telling him, "you say the -ov bit at the end of each name like -*off*."

"Luis Robson's definitely playing up front," Benny went on. Everyone bit their lips to stop themselves from guffawing. The South American striker's name was still the only one that Benny could be sure of pronouncing right.

"How about Shoveov and Pushov?" Narris asked, straight-faced, pronouncing them *Shove-off* and *Push-off*. "Are they in?"

For a moment Benny looked all at sea. The names had got him in such a twist, he simply couldn't tell if these were real ones or not.

"And Buzzov?" Keats Aberdeen chipped in. "How about him?"

"Not forgetting Sentov, Onandov, Runitov and Getemov" added Terry before everyone fell about laughing.

"Yeah, yeah, yeah!" Benny boomed over the

racket. "You can all laugh now. But it won't be so funny when you get out there on the park. I might not know all their names but you mark my words: they're no bunch of jokers. You don't need me to remind you how they stuffed Chelsea at home *and* away in the third round. This is serious stuff tonight, right? *Right?*"

"Right, Boss!" everyone called back – including four new arrivals who suddenly landed in a tangled heap on the floor in their rush to get inside first.

"Sorry I'm late, Boss," gasped shaven-headed left midfielder Chrissie Pick, the club's pin-up boy and occasional fashion model for Versace.

"Sorry too, Boss," chimed the bigger, broader guy wrapped around him. This was his flatmate Madman Mort, the Albion keeper. "We got held up doing a photo-shoot for *Alright, Mate!*"

"*Alright, Mate!*" frowned Terry. "What's that when it's at home?"

"It's this brand new photo-mag," explained Chrissie, getting up and dusting himself down. "All about where people live. It's like *Hello!* – you know?"

Gaffer nodded. "I know *Hello!* That's where the stars invite the cameras into their lovely luxurious homes, right? Then pose with all their flashy furniture?"

"That's the one," Madman told him. "Only

Alright, Mate! is going to be about more –
sort of – ordinary people. Well, yobs really. Like
us."

"So they came to *your* gaff and took
pictures?" asked Luke, open-mouthed. "And
they're going to *publish* them?"

Once, Luke had caught a glimpse inside the
room that Madman and Chrissie shared at their
landlady's house. He'd seen cages at the zoo
that looked in better shape – and smelled quite
a bit better too.

"You got a problem with that?" asked
Madman, pretending to be menacing.

"No, no," Luke said quickly. "I – er – look
forward to seeing the pictures," he smiled.
"Neil Veal fixed it up for you, did he?"

His team-mates nodded. Sleazeball Neil Veal
was their agent. Luke's as well. And he also
represented the other two guys who had just
tumbled into the dressing room: full-backs
Dennis Meldrum and Craig Edwards. "So
where have you pair been then?" Benny asked,
crossing the last names off his blackboard.

"Oh nowhere, Boss," answered Dennis. "We
just got stuck at the end of Chapter Seventeen.
It's all tied up now, though."

Benny shook his head. It was all he could do.
Vealy had somehow got the two defenders a
big publishing deal. Now they had to produce a
steamy novel about babes 'n' soccer by the end

of the season – even though the pair barely knew how to speak, let alone write.

"Get changed quick, all four of you," Benny barked. "And get your minds into *football* gear! Right now! I don't know: photo-shoots and flippin' novels! And opening up new supermarkets every five minutes! In my day there was none of that. We just played the game. We lived football. We ate it, drank it, slept it."

"Yeah, but they hadn't invented cameras back then, had they?" laughed Narris. "There weren't any shops either, were there?"

"What was it *like* – living in the seventeenth century?" grinned Casper Franks.

For all his worries, Benny couldn't help smiling behind his beard. "Just take a look around you," he grunted, "this stadium hasn't changed since about 1600." Then he switched back to serious mode. "Now get yourselves SORTED!"

3

By the time Benny launched into his team-talk, Ash Acre was packed to the rafters. How many frenzied fans were jammed inside? Seventy-six thousand like at Wembley? Fifty-thousand or so like at Old Trafford?

Not likely. The official crowd limit at Albion's cosy little home was just 13,500. And now that some of the concrete steps behind the West End goal had started to crumble, that figure had been lowered, for safety reasons, to under 12,000. It was a good job ITV were showing the game live on television. That way, *all* Albion's fans – old and new alike – could get a look at the action.

Benny's speech didn't last long. "If we don't win this one," he told them, "some of us are gonna be looking for new jobs. You don't need me to tell you that our young Chairman's not the most patient person in the world, and he's *well* gutted by the way we've been playing in the league. It's only our performances in this cup that have stopped 'im from giving half of us the chop. And frankly, I wouldn't blame the guy if he did start wielding the axe. Our form's been diabolical. Up one minute, down the next. We've *gotta* get a bit of consistency going – starting tonight. So go out there in a minute and make those Russkies wish they'd never left their bloomin' igloos!"

There was a short pause as this sank in. Then Gaffer slowly shook his head. "No Boss. It's Eskimos that live in igloos, isn't it?"

"Inuits," nodded Cool Frederick.

"I beg your pardon!" choked Benny, thinking Frederick was giving him abuse.

"Inuits," Frederick repeated. "It's what you gotta call Eskimos now." He clenched a fist. "Maximum respect to the Inuits out there on the ice."

"Well, wherever these Russians have come from," Benny went on. "I want you to go out and make life extremely uncomfortable for them – you got that?"

"*Yes, Boss!*" everyone yelled back. But as the echo of their shouts died away, it went oddly silent in the dressing room. Luke glanced across at Cool F who raised an eyebrow back. For some reason Benny had given the team talk too soon. Usually he sent his lads off up the tunnel with his words of wisdom still ringing in their ears. Now they had a few more minutes just to sit and twiddle their thumbs. Or – in Carl's case – fiddle with his pineapple.

"Oh," said the lanky striker, tossing the spiky fruit over to Craig Edwards. "I almost forgot. Give us a nice whack with that, Craig, will you?"

He stood up, turned round and bent over. All the players, except Craig, clapped their hands over their ears and shut their eyes tight. Then Mr Edwards took careful aim and hurled the pineapple with all his might at Carl's bottom.

"Yaaaaaoooooooohhhh!!!" he bellowed. But then, at once, he straightened up, cleared his throat and thanked Craig. Most footballers have a pre-match ritual of some sort. With Carl, it was having a pineapple thrown at him by Craig. He swore that without the hit, he simply *couldn't* score a goal.

But still it wasn't time for everyone to charge off up the tunnel. Benny looked at his watch, then across at Terry, who kept looking at the door. They both seemed to be expecting something to happen at any moment. Outside on the terraces they could all hear the Albion faithful kicking up a wonderful racket, but in here it was almost creepily quiet.

The silence started to get to Narris. "What's on the telly then, Terry?" he said.

Terry reached across and switched on his little portable set on the physio's bench. Bob Wilson's smiling face swam into view. All around him, Albion fans were chanting and cheering. It was ITV's live transmission from Ash Acre!

"Well, it's absolute bedlam inside this little ground tonight!" Bob told the millions of viewers. "But can plucky Albion succeed where Chelsea failed before them? That's the question. And it's one that Gary Newbon put, earlier today, to Albion's young Chairman, head of the fabulously successful Majestic Software empire: schoolboy computer wizard James 'Jimbo' Prince..."

The floodlit chaos inside Ash Acre was replaced on-screen by a bird's-eye view of a state-of-the-art stadium in the middle of a huge building site. "This is the soon-to-be-completed Majestic Stadium," came Gary's Newbon's voice-over. "In under a month's time, James Prince hopes to make *this* the home of the club that he bought – lock, stock and barrel – at the end of last season." The picture changed again. Now a nerdy-looking kid with glasses and corkscrew hair filled the screen. "Jimbo: you've built this place phenomenally quickly..."

"I'd like to disagree with you there," the nerd interrupted in an angry, high-pitched voice. "If I'd had *my* way, this whole stadium complex would have been fully operational before last Christmas. The builders have let me down time and again." He narrowed his eyes. "But they won't let me down any more – or I'll sue them till the pips squeak. So I assure you that we *will* be playing the home leg of our UEFA Cup semi-final here in our new home. We *will* be!"

"*Semi*-final?" gulped Gary Newbon. "Isn't there the little matter of beating Spartak Moscow in the *quarter*-final first?"

James Prince didn't even answer that. He just narrowed his eyes even more.

"So you're confident about tonight's game then, James?" Gary went on. "But won't it be an uphill struggle for Albion without your star striker?"

James Prince looked at the camera as if he'd just been booted on both knees. "If you're talking about Dogan Mezir, I am *not* prepared to discuss that matter!"

"But James – er – Mr Prince, surely the Armenian goal-machine is vital to your success in this cup? I mean, after his stunning display against Bayern in the last round..."

"I am *not* prepared to discuss this matter!" Jimbo repeated grimly.

"I can see it must be embarrassing for you," Gary Newbon battled on, "paying all that money for a striker who plays just one brilliant game, then has to return to Armenia to sort out a problem with the family's sheep flock. But when are we likely to see him in an Albion shirt again? Mr Prince? *Mr Prince...?*"

The screen no longer showed the young

computer-whiz's face. Instead it showed his back as he furiously stalked off. And it can't have been easy for someone on crutches to stalk off so furiously – but Princey managed it.

"James Prince, there," Bob Wilson smiled, back at Ash Acre. "Not only Albion's Chairman, but sometimes one of their players as well. But as you can see, injury has again kept him out of the Albion line-up tonight. Earlier this week he suffered his *fourth* training accident of the season when he collided with defender Dennis Meldrum..."

In the Albion dressing room, everyone murmured their thanks to Dennis for taking Jimbo out. Dennis shrugged modestly. For although Jimbo was a true star at software, at soccer he really stank. Not that he was ever likely to admit that. And – since he owned the club – he made it clear to Benny that whenever he was fit, he expected to play. So the other players just had to make sure that his health was never quite a hundred per cent. It was a dirty job but somebody had to do it, and this week it had been Dennis' turn.

Suddenly the door burst open and two burly minders in penguin suits stomped in to left and right. Then a much smaller figure limped in between them, paused to push the door shut with one of his crutches, then glared down at the squad.

"Jimbo!" cried Benny, forcing a smile and glancing yet again at his watch.

"We was wondering where you'd got to," said Terry, switching off the TV.

Luke curled his toes inside his trainers. (His mum had never let him try on boots, and now it was too late to get used to playing in a pair.) So *this* is what we've been waiting for, he thought glumly: an earful from the chairman.

But Luke was wrong – at least to begin with.

For what felt like an hour, Jimbo just kept glaring. Everyone sat at attention, waiting for an outburst. His glasses were so thick, you never quite knew who he was looking at. And he always looked so *stroppy*. It amazed Luke that a kid who had made so much money hardly ever seemed to smile. He wasn't really a bad bloke when you got to know him. But if things didn't go just the way he wanted them to – whoa, could he throw a wobbler!

"OK, men," he piped in the end, surprisingly quietly. "I've asked Benny to leave a few moments free before you go out tonight. There's somebody waiting outside that I want you all to listen to. His name is Alan Wilkie and he's a 'motivational speaker'. That's someone who goes around giving talks to businessmen – firing them up for the challenges they face in their jobs. I believe that he can fire *you* all up too, for the task ahead tonight. After all, football's pretty similar to business. It's all about mental strength – getting your mind right, then really going for it. And this guy sure does know how to get people's minds right." He nodded at a minder. "Tell Mr Wilkie we're ready for him."

As the players exchanged baffled looks, the minder went back outside. Benny was looking pretty glum. Luke could guess why. It was a *manager*'s job to get his players going before a big match. By bringing in this "motivational speaker", Jimbo was interfering with all the Bossman's own preparations. Just like he'd interfered by letting a fly-on-the-wall documentary TV crew film Benny's every move outside the safety of the dressing room.

After a short pause the door opened again and the minder returned, alone, looking down uncertainly at a scrap of paper with some writing on it.

"I said we're *ready*," Jimbo snarled, clenching his little fists.

"Well – er – there's been a bit of a hitch, sir," stammered the minder, still staring at the scribbled note.

"Hitch! What *hitch*?"

"Mr Wilkie, sir. He's, well, he says he's lost his voice."

"*Says* he's lost his voice?" Jimbo screeched back. "How can he *say* that?"

Sheepishly the minder waved the bit of paper. "He wrote it down for me, sir."

"Oh *did* he?" Jimbo's little face had gone purple with fury. "Well, he's had £2,500 from me *in advance* for coming here to do this job!" The players looked at each other, gobsmacked at the huge amount. "So you tell him to get himself in here *pronto*! If he can't say his stuff he can flipping well *mime* it!"

And he meant it! The players were all fighting back smiles when the door opened once more. In strutted a tall, oldish guy in combat gear and with a very embarrassed look on his craggy face. Without daring to cast a glance at Jimbo, he started playing the weirdest game of charades Luke had ever known.

First he clenched his teeth and crossed his hands over his chest. When everyone just looked puzzled, he waved his hands, encouraging them to call out. Then he put his hands back on his chest, as if he was holding a baby.

"Baby?" suggested Gaffer with a shrug. Mr Wilkie shook his head, wincing.

"Pain?" asked Craig. A harder headshake from Mr Wilkie.

"Heart!" cried Terry triumphantly, as Mr Wilkie nodded with relief. Then he pointed at everyone, tapped his heart, and shook his fist.

"We've got to rip our own hearts out?" queried Carl, looking worried.

"Nah! He means we've got to show heart and *fight*," Chrissie corrected him. "Right?"

Mr Wilkie nodded frantically, then snatched up a bottle from Terry's bag.

"Foul-smelling stuff that Tel rubs on our muscles!" said Half-Fat.

Mr Wilkie just held it higher and pointed hard at it, then at them.

"You think we stink?" guessed Casper Franks. No, no, no.

"I've got it – *bottle*!" grinned Madman. "I'm getting the hang of this now. We've all got to show a bit of bottle!" Mr Wilkie gave him the thumbs-up. Then, to everyone's surprise, he dropped down on to all fours, threw back his head and seemed to be miming a howl up at the dressing-room ceiling.

"We're so bad, it makes you want to get down and weep?" asked Keats.

No.

Mr Wilkie put one hand behind him and began to shake it about like a tail.

"Is it a song or a film?" enquired Dennis, who clearly hadn't understood what was going on here at all. "Animal?" said Luke. Yes! More mock-howling from Mr Wilkie. Calls now came in from all sides: "Wolf!" "Hyena!" "*Dog!*" Right!

Then Mr Wilkie rolled over on his back and stuck his legs and "paws" in the air.

"Dead dog!" No. "Dog is dead!" No. "*Our* Dog?" Yes!

"Our Dog's dead?" said Narris in alarm as Mr

Wilkie sprang to his feet and made a *so what?* gesture with his hands. "How did it happen? When?"

"No," sighed Chrissie, stifling a yawn. "I think he means we don't *need* Dog tonight. We might *think* we'll be lost without him, but actually it doesn't matter. As long as we show heart, fight and bottle, we'll be all right."

Everyone, including Mr Wilkie, looked at the young slaphead in awe. And, because his answer was spot-on, they gave him a round of applause. Chrissie just shrugged. "I'm red hot at this game," he said. "When you've had as many foreign girlfriends as me, you learn how to communicate in ... other ways."

At that point Jimbo decided he'd had enough. He limped forward and pushed Mr Wilkie back towards the door with one of his crutches. "All right, all right," he snapped. "That'll do. You lot," he pointed a crutch at the squad, "get out there now and do it for Castle Albion. You're good enough. I know it. You know it. Now *prove* it!" He turned on Mr Wilkie. "And as for you, you owe me a refund!"

"OK, lads," cried Benny, looking a bit happier now. "You heard the Chairman – let's go give these Russians a seeing-to! Straight from the *Kickov*!"

5

The atmosphere out in the stadium was electric. Only someone who really didn't like football would not have felt the tingles. Someone, Luke thought, like his own mum. But he had to put her right out of his mind for the next hour and a half. He and his ten team-mates had a major mission to accomplish here.

But when he glanced across the halfway line at the strangers from Spartak, *they* were clearly charged up too. While Gaffer shook hands with their skipper, the rest of them were doing all sorts of tricks with their practice balls. The way some of them were juggling, flipping and flicking they looked as if they could have earned a decent living in the Moscow State Circus.

Luke was very impressed. So were Albion's hardcore fans who stood on the South Side terrace. Led by Supporters Club Chairman Rocky Mitford, they boomed a great "Olé!" every time one of the red-and-whites pulled off a little piece of magic with the ball. The players in turn waved back. It must have been nice for them to have *some* support away from home – even if the match hadn't yet started. Only a few hundred of their own fans had been able to make the long trip. And after all those hours and miles, there they were – huddled behind the Town End goal, with no roof above them to keep off the drizzle.

"Tonight," crackled the tannoy, "we are proud to welcome to Ash Acre the players, supporters and officials of *Spartak Moscow*!"

A wave of applause for the visitors swept round the stadium. Or maybe the home fans were just celebrating the fact that for the first time that season, the stadium announcer had said a whole sentence without some sort of technical problem with the tannoy making mincemeat of his words.

"The Spartak line-up tonight will be as follows…" he went on. And now a peculiar hush fell. That was *two* perfectly clear sentences in a row. A miracle! "In goal … Alexandr Flo-sorry-Filoman-no-Fil*i*mon-ov. I'll repeat that: ahem – *Alexandr Filimonov*. At number three, Dim-or rather-Dum-no-I-was-right-first-time-D*imi*tri er, um, Kresta-no-that-should-be-Klesta-with-an-'l'-oh-no-it's Khlest*ov*. Yes! Dimitry Khlest*ov*! I do apologize for this. And at number six…"

And so it went on. In agonies of embarrass-ment, the announcer stumbled his way through

25

the entire team until he breathed with enormous relief: "And finally, at number twenty four: Luis Robson!" A hearty cheer greeted the one name that he'd been able to get right. He didn't bother with the Spartak subs (the kick-off was already two minutes late by now) but went straight on to the Albion line up. "In goal, number one: M... *plink, kerplunk*, buzzzzzzzz..."

The system just couldn't keep coping. Off it went and off it stayed for the rest of the night. Luke couldn't help grinning across at Frederick. How that announcer must have wished it had gone dead just a few minutes earlier!

But now the only sound that rang out came from the ref's puckered lips. With one blast from his whistle, the home side's first ever UEFA Cup quarter-final got under way. Albion, thought Luke: your ninety minutes start *now*!

And, for the first twenty of them, the Russians went for broke. Luke was surprised. Normally in these two-legged ties, the away team played it very cagey. Albion did when they were away – or at least, they tried to – taking the heat out of the game, slowing things down, taking no risks.

The art of a good European away performance, Benny kept telling them, was simply not to lose: "Draw the away leg, win the home one, Bob's your uncle – into the hat for the next round!"

Plainly these Russians didn't agree.

Luke and his mates used to say "Next Goal Wins It" when a park game had been going on for too long and some of the kids had to get home for tea. Right from the off here, Spartak seemed to be playing "*First* Goal Wins It". And, in a way, they had a point. For a precious away goal counted double in this competition, and that could make all the difference in the end.

The visitors came forward mob-handed. Hitting Madman's bar, grazing his left-hand post, peppering his six-yard box with crosses, bringing the absolute defensive best out of Craig, Gaffer, Dennis and – as always – Cool Frederick. For minutes on end, Albion just couldn't seem to get the ball off them. Carl and Keats barely had a touch in the entire first quarter. Heart, fight and bottle didn't come into it. First, by hook or by crook, they had to win possession.

Over on the bench, Benny was not pleased. "Get *among* them!" Luke heard him yell more than once. "Put yourselves about a bit! Get stuck *in*!"

Now that was always a dodgy bit of advice to give to midfield battlers like Narris Phiz and Half-Fat Milkes. Neither was the most gifted ball-player in professional football. Even in their dreams they couldn't perform pre-match tricks like those Spartakists. But, in the words of John Motson during the last year's FA Cup Final, they did both "like a tussle". And now their boss was ordering them to go into fight mode. Luke feared the worst – and got it.

It all went off in the twenty-third minute. The Russian number twenty-one, whose name *didn't* end in "-ov" (unless they couldn't fit the whole of it on to his shirt) received a pass ten yards inside the Albion half. Spinning away from Chrissie, he saw Narris making a bee-line straight for him. He possibly also felt the turf tremble as Half-Fat stormed at him from behind.

Not wanting to be crushed in an Albion sandwich, he made as if to spray a pass out to the left. Then he checked and knocked it sideways to a team-mate on the right instead. But it didn't really matter *which* direction he'd chosen. Narris had already decided to make a lunge at him. Luke screwed up his face as the Tussler from Trinidad launched himself horizontally through the air.

Late tackle? You have to be joking! This one was so late, the groundstaff had switched off the lights and gone home by the time Narris clattered into his man.

There was such a sharp intake of breath from the whole of the South Side that Luke felt himself being sucked slightly backwards. The ref was reaching into his pocket for a card even before his whistle-blast for the foul had ended.

It didn't look good for Mr Phiz. It didn't look good at all.

6

Narris acted the innocent, of course. That's all part and parcel of the modern game. Play the executioner, then act the innocent.

He even tried to haul the poleaxed number twenty-one back on to his feet. But he would have needed a crane for that – and then a bag for all the bits that had broken off under the impact. This was a five-star stretcher job. Luke wondered what the poor crocked Russian would think of English hospital food. Most of the crowd must have been thinking the same thing. They were deathly quiet.

Meanwhile the ref – a skinny little bloke from Greece with a Charlie Chaplin moustache – was taking an age to sort out his cards. Why do refs do that so often? Why don't they keep the red card in one pocket, the yellow in the other?

But Narris knew he didn't have a prayer on this one. Any moment now he was going to see red, so he decided to head straight for the tunnel anyway. He was stepping on to the cinder track when a huge shout went up all round the ground. On three sides it was one of amazement and relief. On the fourth, behind the Town End goal, it was one of amazement and absolute fury (but the sound of those few hundred Spartak fans was completely drowned out).

The ref was holding up only a yellow card!

Everyone from the stretcher-carriers to Benny Webb on the touchline waited for the skinny little man to realize his mistake. But realize it, he did not. In fact, he seemed to have *chosen* yellow instead of red. Quite unflustered, he jotted down N Phiz's name and number in his notebook, put away his cards, then watched the poor old number twenty-one – Bezrodny – being carried out of the fray. The Russians around him went potty protesting, but he paid not the slightest heed.

All of which left Narris looking very bewildered. Blinking back over his shoulder – with one foot on the cinder track and one foot still on the pitch – he couldn't believe his luck.

"Get your tail back in here!" Gaffer yelled over at him, waving hard.

"He must have let you stay on cos you didn't actually decapitate the guy," laughed Chrissie as Narris trotted past him again.

"Talk about the Great Escape," grinned Half-Fat. "Is the ref your long-lost dad or something?"

But once the game got going again, the Albion players stopped smirking. The crowd wised up to it first, and they voiced their dismay in no uncertain terms. For it seemed that the ref *had*, after all, decided to punish that Fearsome Foul harshly. Not by sending Narris off for an early bath – but by giving every decision for the next twenty-two minutes in Spartak's favour.

It started with Carl being fingered for offside six times. Not once did the referee's assistant raise his flag. It was all down to the man in yellow. Then Keatso was done for handball just inside the Albion half – though everyone could see he'd used his chest to bring a lofted pass from Luke under control.

From there on in, it was all downhill. Whenever a home player breathed near a Spartakist, *blast!* went the whistle. To be fair to the Russians, they didn't milk the situation. There was no Oscar-winning diving and writhing from them. They in turn couldn't believe their own luck now. But fortunately for Albion, none of the free kicks gifted to them led to goal-threatening incidents.

That was mainly due to some masterly positional play from Cool Frederick. Knowing that he couldn't afford to get too close to the Spartak strikers, he kept track of them by his own personal radar. Time after time he intercepted passes long before they reached their intended destinations. Reading the game? It was almost as if he could read the *minds* of these Russians.

As the half neared its end, he made one particularly fine cut-out on the edge of the Albion box. Darting forward to cushion the ball on his thigh, he didn't let it touch the deck before looping it up into the visitors half for Luke to run on to.

The pass was perfectly weighted – rolling to a standstill just between Luke and the oncoming Spartak number three. Quick as a flash, Luke pushed it to one side of him, ran around the other – and found himself in acres of space with only the keeper to beat!

"Go Lukey! Go Lukey!"

roared every English voice in the stadium. They knew that the Studless Sensation gobbled up chances like this for breakfast.

But, sadly for him, he'd got up too late for breakfast that day.

At least, that's what the ref decided. As Luke fooled the keeper into spreading himself leftwards and shaped to hit it high into the net to his right, *blast! blast! blast!* went the half-time whistle.

"Blast! Blast! Blast!"

screamed 11,000-odd Albion fans (or words to that effect). The ref hadn't added on a *second* of injury time. And everyone knew there had been plenty of that, thanks to Narris's Nightmare Nobbler. But there was no point in the players making a song and dance about it. For better or worse, the referee's decision was final. Off they all trooped for some sweet tea and a shedload of stroppy remarks from their long-suffering manager.

"What on *earth* d'you call that tackle then, Narris?" he fumed.

"Fashionably late?" suggested Madman.

"I'll give you fashion!" Benny growled. "You haven't got your minds on the job in hand, half of you! They're all over you. They've got more hunger, more appetite, more *everything*! I'm amazed you're not three down already!"

"Me too," sighed Carl. "But the ref's not actually allowed to *score* for them, is he?"

"No," agreed Keatso, "but he'll probably wear a red-and-white shirt for the second half. He's been on their side ever since Narris clipped their bloke. How come we've got a ref from Greece anyway? That's right next to Russia, innit?"

"Never you mind where Greece is," stormed Benny, plainly not sure where it was himself. "You can beat this bunch of Russians *and* you can beat this ref!" He looked down and saw a glint come into Narris's eye. "No, no! I don't mean beat him *physically*! I do wonder about you at times, Narris son."

7

The ref was still wearing yellow as the second forty-five began. Maybe a UEFA official had bawled him out during the interval. Or perhaps he'd tuned in to watch Bob Wilson and Terry Venables taking apart his performance on ITV. Whatever the reason, he now treated both teams in exactly the same way – unfairly.

Gradually it dawned on the players and fans alike that he wasn't favouring one side over the other. He was just a very, very bad referee. His main aim seemed to be to blow his whistle whenever the game threatened to start to flow. The slightest nudge or brush got him puffing. He would give a blast at foul throws, free-kicks taken just inches away from the correct spot, or even – in the case of Dennis Meldrum – for "looking at me in a funny way" ... three times.

Stop-start, stop-start, stop-start. If ITV had edited together a soundtrack of his second-half stoppages afterwards, they would have ended up with a shrill little symphony lasting the best part of half an hour. And Luke hoped the ref was enjoying it, because nobody else in the ground was. Until the seventy-fourth minute, that was.

Amazingly, the whole of that minute went by without a whistle-blast. It started with an Albion throw-in on the left. Albion were now attacking the Town End, and the ball rolled into touch right in front of the Albion dug-out. Terry V shot out, scooped it up and tossed it to Craig Edwards.

Craig went to take a quick throw – looking first at the ref in case Terry had done something illegal. Miracle of miracles, he hadn't. Craig's long throw infield fell right into the path of Cool F who was striding up elegantly from the back. Without needing to break stride, he chipped up a delightful little ball, at head height, to the edge of the Spartak penalty area.

That was where Keats Aberdeen was waiting – with the Russian number five breathing down his neck as he had been all night. Up they both went – Keatso trying to flick it on, his marker trying to head it clear. Even as he leapt, Keats took a look at the ref, and made a point of keeping his arms tight in to his sides, just in case he got blown up for high elbows. Somehow that seemed to give him a bit of extra spring. He got to the ball first, and glanced a neat little header to his left.

The nearest oncoming Albion man was Half-Fat. He was twenty-five yards out. The ball was sitting up nicely, and he fancied his chances with a shot. So he slowed down a pace, took stock of the goal ahead, and steadied himself to let rip. But, however carefully he lined his shot up, Milkesey wasn't really the Albion player you wanted in this situation. The local *Evening Argus* statistics told their own sorry story of his season so far in front of goal. *Milkes, M: Shots on target – 4; Shots off target – 37; Goals scored 0*. He was a great team man in all sorts of ways – if you cut him he bled blue and white – but his appearances on the scoresheet were very few and far between.

Which was why, on this vital occasion, he froze as a voice called behind him: "Leave it, Milkesey! Let it roll! It's Luke's ball!" The shout had come from Luke himself, who was tearing up diagonally towards the box. And the older midfielder did just what he was told – letting the ball roll tantalizingly in front of him, with his leg still coiled back in readiness to shoot and miss.

Dummy of the season? No contest!

The Spartak keeper didn't stand a chance as Luke suddenly popped into view from behind Half-Fat to unleash a ferocious, unstoppable cross-shot into the top right-hand corner of his net.

The ref could have disallowed it for any number of reasons. Which would he choose? Cruelty to leather? Hitting a shot in trainers with more power than any normal person had a right to? Making the Russian international goal-keeper look embarrassingly flat-footed? He took none of these options. But he got to blow his whistle anyway – as he blasted away while raising one arm to point back to the centre-spot and signal Albion's opening goal of the evening!

They'd done it. The English minnows were ahead! Luke turned and leapt into the waiting arms of Half-Fat to salute his perfect goal-assist. Seconds later eight other men in blue hoops were piling on top of them with their own individual votes of thanks.

The ref wasn't having any of that. *Blast! Blast! Blast! Blast!* He peeled off each Albion player personally, blowing his beloved whistle right into their ears. If you ever needed a party to be pooped, this really was the guy to call.

But the Albion players weren't bothered. Nor were their wildly happy fans. There was noth-ing the man in black could do to stop *their* celebrations. And within three minutes of the restart, they had a chance to go through it all again.

This time, the build-up was nowhere near as slick as before. Narris dispossessed the Spartak number eighteen in the centre-circle, but then scuffed his short sideways pass to Chrissie. The Bald Bombshell had to make a lunge to scoop away the ball before the number eighteen could get it back. Skidding in, he hooked it low and hard into the Spartak half.

Two visiting defenders, taken unawares, could only watch as the ball bulleted between them. Carl was a bit quicker off the mark. Darting between them too, he gave chase and suddenly – just like Luke at the end of the first half – he found himself in a one-on-one with Filimonov in the Spartak goal.

The keeper dashed out to narrow the angle. But Carl never bothered much about things like angles. Roared on by Rocky and Co, he let fly in the general direction of the goal. It wasn't one of his better efforts. The keeper had got his sums right. The ball thudded into his shins. But then it bounced invitingly back out – giving the Pineapple Goal-Poacher a second bite at the cherry.

Carl lashed it goalwards once again. The keeper leapt acrobatically to fist it over the bar. That night, however, the bar was not his friend. The ball cannoned against its underside, crashed down on to the goal-line, bounced up again – and by that stage Carl had surged past the despairing keeper to nod it finally into the net.

Messy, yes. But quite magnificent too. Carl certainly thought so. As soon as he'd checked that the ref had given the goal, he turned to his team and – before they could dive on him – he gave his own personal tribute to their motivational speaker. First he crossed his hands over his heart. Then he raised a fist. Then with both hands he made the curvy shape of a bottle in the air.

"You love smashing bottles?" Luke heard Dennis asking, baffled, as they fell on the scorer. All around the ground joyful Albion fans were already copying the new routine, while hurling great inflatable pineapples up into the air.

Albion two Spartak nil! That was a scoreline Benny and his boys would happily have settled for before Kickov. All they had to do now was play out time. Which they did, highly success-fully – and mostly in Spartak's half, right up to the last minute of the game.

That minute lasted a very long time. The whistle-happy ref, of course, had his dummy-substitute in his mouth for the whole of it. He was obviously building up for a mega triple-blast to round off the game. And as Albion knocked the ball back and forth without a care, the first long note rang out. The crowd went wild at once, drowning out any sound the ref was making. Most of the Albion players turned to one another in glee and starting their high-fiving and hugging.

"We're on our way to Rom-a!"

sang the whole stadium – apart from the sulky-looking souls behind the Town End goal – since the UEFA Cup final was scheduled to be played in Rome's magnificent Olympic Stadium. Some of the more excitable players joined in. They thought it was all over. But as Luke now plainly saw, it wasn't.

"No, no!" he tried to bawl at the others. "He's only given a free kick! *Look!*" But nobody heard him. Nobody saw that the ref had just given Keatso offside. Yet one or two of them did see the Russians hump a quick free-kick forward, to where the easily pronounceable Luis Robson was standing well offside himself.

Sadly the ref didn't notice this last fact. And before anyone in the Albion defence could say "We wuz robbed", the Russians' Robbo looped a shot high over Madman's head and into the gaping net. Three whistle-blasts was the rotten ref's only response. Game over. And although no one could believe it, the Russian "goal" stood. Albion two, Spartak one was going to be the final result.

Right there at the death, the Russkies had clawed their way back into the tie. They now had a magical away goal – and none of the endless appeals from Benny, his squad and Albion's disgusted fans could do anything to change Mr Puffy Cheeks' mind about it.

He needed an escort of six policemen as he

left Ash Acre that night. Nobody touched him. No one could get close enough. But he went back to Greece with over 11,000 suggestions as to what he could do with his whistle.

8

"Hey man, what a bummer – conceding in the very last minute! And on the TV pictures I saw over here, that Russian dude looked *way* offside!"

Luke, still gutted from the result, nodded into the phone. "I know, Dad. It was – er – a bit of a disappointment." He couldn't say any more than that. His mum was hovering just outside the sitting room while he had this early-morning chat with his father. *She* still thought he'd been around at Cool F's doing German revision the night before. And if she caught even the slightest whiff of a football conversation here, the whole house would go on Wobbler Alert.

"That was a groovy goal you put away though, Lukey," his dad went on from faraway Alice Springs where it was now late afternoon.

He was an ageing-hippie pop musician who called himself TAFKAG (The Artist Formerly Known As Green), and was yet another client of

Neil Veal's. For years he'd enjoyed so little success that you could have crammed all his fans into the boot of a Metro and still had room for a spare tyre. Then suddenly he had struck gold in some of the world's oddest spots with "Castle Rap" – a single he'd cut with Cool Frederick to celebrate Albion's FA Cup Final appearance at Wembley. Now he spent almost all his time on tour, although not always in the most glamorous of places. Currently he seemed to be doing the rounds of sheep-shearing stations in the remotest parts of Australia. "How many goals have you scored this season now?" he went on. "Fourteen?"

"Um – something like that," Luke murmured, glancing over his shoulder to see if his mum was still within hearing range. She wasn't. But someone else was: his stepdad, Rodney – standing in the doorway with an anxious expression on his pale, bespectacled face. When he caught Luke's eye, he waved urgently and began to mouth a question which Luke couldn't quite understand.

"Hold on a minute, Dad," Luke said softly. "Rodney's trying to say something."

His stepdad – who, like TAFKAG, loved football just about as much as his mum hated it – leaned further into the room and hissed: "Ask him how he's planning to get you to Moscow for the second leg."

Luke nodded. "Oh yeah, dad." He lowered his voice. "There's the – um – problem of – er – *the Thursday after next.*"

Briefly there was silence. Then the light-bulb went on in TAFKAG's slightly out-of-it head. "Oh, I've got you sussed! The away leg in Moscow?"

"Right." Luke nodded across at Rodney who was craning his neck to try and listen in – even though his mum was making an awful din washing up frying pans in the kitchen. (Luke's mum's breakfasts were always a lot stronger on sound than taste.) "Have you had any ideas, then?"

"No sweat, man," Luke's dad assured him. "I'm on the case. Next Tuesday I'll be back in the Land of the Brits. Just a one-week stopover between this set of dates down under and my next mini-tour of northern Scandinavia. But tell your mum I'll come and rap with her then and get it all squared up. I've already promised Benny you'll *definitely* be on that plane a week on Tuesday with the rest of the squad. So trust me Lukey, you will be."

"But *how*, Dad?" Luke couldn't help pressing him under the frying-pan racket. His dad had often helped him in the past to get to league fixtures in places like Plymouth, Carlisle and Halifax. But Moscow really was a bit further afield.

"Gotta run now, Lukey," he said. "I'm getting

a signal from the sound engineers. We're laying down a backing track for a brand new single right out here in the outback – dingo noises and everything! Should be ready just in time for Albion's appearance at the UEFA Cup final in Rome! *Ciao* for now!"

Dingo noises? Luke put down the phone and shrugged up at his stepdad. "He's coming here on Tuesday," Luke whispered. "He says there won't be a problem."

Rodney blinked, then held up both hands with his fingers tightly crossed. Albion were really going to need Luke for the second leg. Their lead was so slim and – of course – Spartak had that away goal too. But now he wouldn't know for another five days if he'd be going or not.

As TAFKAG had said, the Albion squad were booked on to a flight from Heathrow in two Tuesdays' time. Benny had insisted that they arrive in Moscow two whole days before the match, to get themselves "acclimaterized", as he put it. He seemed to think they would be needing snowploughs just to travel from their hotel to the Lokomotiv stadium where Spartak played – even though Frederick kept on telling him that March was actually pretty mild in Moscow.

Before then, however, Albion had another big crunch game. Tomorrow afternoon, to be precise:

against Torquay United – all the way down in Devon. Luke's club was still hungry for Division Three points, yet there was no way that *he* could help to put them in the bag, thanks as usual to his mum.

Two days before, she had decided the family needed a new house. Not a bigger one, necessarily. A house the same size would do – just as long as it had a *much* bigger garden. Planting, seeding, pruning, clipping, trimming, watering, hoeing, dibbing, weeding, raking, manuring – these were the activities that made Mrs Green's heart beat faster. But in the garden they had at the moment, there simply wasn't enough scope for her. So now they had to move house. And Saturday had been set aside for her, Rodney and Luke to start checking out what the estate agents had to offer. Luke could barely contain his excitement!

"Have you finished nattering on in there, Luke?" she snapped through. Anyone would have thought *she* had to pay for TAFKAG's frequent calls from abroad. "You'd better get off to school now. Oh, and good luck with the German test."

"German test?" Luke called back, his head still full of football.

"The one you were *revising* for last night," Rodney popped his head around the door to remind him.

"Oh, the *German test* – right." Luke called back. "Yeah – thanks. Frederick and I really revised our socks off last night." Then he added under his breath: "And I really, really hope that, at the end of the day, we get the right result."

9

Poor Albion didn't get the right result at Torquay on Saturday. But it wasn't exactly the wrong result either. In several of the houses Luke trekked around, the owners were listening to local radio which was running live commentary on the game. His mum didn't look too pleased about that, and Luke had to pretend not to be listening, but he managed to catch a few significant soundbites.

It didn't seem like a vintage match. Albion probably had a bit of a European hangover from Thursday night, while Torquay were just going through one of their regular poor patches. The two teams cancelled each other out on a boggy Plainmoor pitch, and had to make do with a point each from a drab nil-nil draw. That wasn't much use to Albion. Their match the following Saturday had been postponed to let them prepare for the Spartak away leg. So by the time they played again in the league, they could well be propping up the table.

Meanwhile Luke didn't exactly have the time of his life house-hunting. If you've seen one "pebble-dashed semi-detached home in need of some modernization with a ninety-foot garden of great potential", you've seen them all. He went on auto-pilot after house number four. Rodney looked pretty glazed as well. But Luke's mum was in seventh heaven. She certainly had a vivid imagination. Every scruffy bit of lawn she inspected was transformed in her mind into a miniature Kew Gardens, complete with ornamental lakes, hanging bridges and flower-filled hothouses. All Luke could do was vaguely map out in his mind where two sets of goalposts might be erected.

There were even more addresses to check out on Sunday – so Luke was pretty thrilled to get back to school on Monday. That might sound odd, but over the past term, Luke's Mondays hadn't been like most other schoolboys'.

His lessons lasted only from nine until ten, then a taxi arrived in the staff car-park to whisk him off to Ash Acre for training. This arrangement had the full blessing of his headmistress. In fact, she was the one who had suggested it.

A lifelong Albion season-ticket holder, she thought Luke's studies wouldn't be harmed by one – or sometimes even two – training sessions per week. Needless to say, Luke's mum knew nothing about any of this. The head had also helped Luke to get to the UEFA Cup away leg in Munich by fixing up an exchange trip for him with a family she knew in Germany.

"You've got it all to do in Moscow now, haven't you?" she asked with a frown as Luke passed her office on his way out to the taxi. "And I can't see any way that *I* can get you to Russia and back. Has your dad had any bright ideas?"

"He says he's working on it, Miss," Luke told her. "He's going to tackle my mum on Tuesday."

The head seemed to flinch, then slowly she nodded her head. "I wish him luck there. Now off you go, but make sure you're back in good time for Physics."

When Luke arrived in the Home Team dressing-room at Ash Acre, everyone else – including Cool F – was already changed. If Luke's school timetable was a little weird, his mate's was from another planet altogether. Young Mr Dulac, who lived with his older sister, wasn't just gifted with two great feet; he had a gigantic brain as well. There was so little that the staff at Luke's school could teach him that they let him come and go as he chose. He still got A-star grades for most of his work, while *also* running a rare records search business from home, collaborating musically with TAFKAG (*and* generally being just so cool that you could have made ice-cubes in his belly-button).

"All right, Luke?" Benny cried from over by the blackboard. "I've had a chat with your dad. He seems quite confident he'll be able to get you to Moscow."

"Touch wood," replied Luke, patting Dennis' head as he went past to his peg.

"Get changed quick then, son," Benny told him. "And listen up the rest of you – I've got a bit of news for you all."

"Oh, don't tell us!" groaned Craig. "They've asked you to manage England?"

"Or Jimbo's decided he's going to play in Moscow," suggested Madman, "injury or no injury?"

"It wouldn't make much difference either way," grunted Half-Fat. "He might play *better* on crutches. Or maybe even with both legs chopped off?"

"Now *there's* a thought," mused Narris.

"No, no," said Benny. "It's nothin' to do with Jimbo. Or rather – in a roundabout way – I suppose you could say that it *is*."

"Come on, Boss," sighed Gaffer. "The suspense is killing us. Spit it out."

"OK, OK," smiled Benny. "Hold on to your hamstrings. Are you ready now... *The Dog's on his way back!*"

"*Noooooooooooooooooooooo!*" cried everyone. "*Really?*"

"Yeah – really!" Benny chirped back, as each

player's grin widened. Maybe, like Luke, they were all remembering Dogan Mezir's awesome debut in the Olympic Stadium to clinch victory over Bayern Munich. None of them had ever seen a man move so fast or shoot so hard. He was clearly different class but, after that one game, nobody at the club had seen hide nor hair of him. This was because back in his native Armenia he was a shepherd and, in his absence, his beloved flock had suddenly gone missing.

Dog had returned at once to try to track the animals down. He seemed to be involved in some kind of inter-family conflict. The sheep had been stolen, but each week Dog managed to find a few more until now, at last, Benny could announce to his thrilled team-mates: "His whole flock is back in place!"

"That's brilliant, Boss," said Chrissie. "But where does Jimbo come into it?"

"Well," Benny replied, "after last Thursday, Jimbo decided that the Dog *had* to play in the return leg. So he sent Neil Veal over to Armenia to read him the riot act and tell him to get on his bike. That's when Vealy found that the sheep crisis was over. He gave me a ring about it this morning. And the two of them are setting straight off for Moscow as we speak!"

"The Dog..." said Casper Franks hesitantly, "...and *Vealy*?"

"Well, he is the lad's agent," said Benny. "But

yes, I must admit – it doesn't sound like a very promising pairing. I've just got to trust them, though, haven't I? Vealy swore he'd deliver the Dog on time. In fact he said that if he didn't get him on to that pitch in Moscow, he would drink his own weight in vodka."

The bubbly mood in the dressing room suddenly went a bit flat. It was hardly surprising. The Dog was a simple soul. He didn't speak a word of English. (No, he spoke seven: *I am exceedingly pleased to meet you* – over and over and over.) And before the Bayern game he'd never travelled more than twenty miles from his home village. The main reason for this was that he refused point-blank to travel by powered transport. Dennis Bergkamp said no to aeroplanes. The Dog did too. But he also said it to cars, lorries, motorbikes, mopeds, buses, coaches, trams, hovercrafts, motor-boats, cruise-liners...

Terry had managed to get him from his homeland to Munich on a tandem. But Terry was a pretty reliable bloke. Now Vealo had to do the same thing, from Armenia to Moscow. And reliable was not a word that anyone *ever* used about Neil Veal. As an agent, he lived to make money. If he saw a chance along the route to "develop" his client's "commercial potential", he would take it. And if he couldn't see a chance, he would shift heaven and earth to create one.

"Let's just hope," sighed Gaffer, "that there aren't too many supermarkets they want opening on the road to Moscow."

"They don't *have* supermarkets over there, do they?" smiled Ruel Bibbo, ex-Albion striker and now chief executive of the club's Soccer Academy.

"What's that?" asked Carl, looking up sharply. "They must have Marks and Spencers, right? *Everywhere* has Marks and Spencers."

"You gotta be joking," Terry chuckled back. "Marks and Spencers in Russa!"

"But that's where I get my pineapples from!" wailed Carl, a look of real panic on his face now. "I've got to be able to get a pineapple before the game!"

"We'll sort you out a pineapple over there, son," Benny assured him. "Don't you worry." But Carl didn't look convinced. Not one bit.

"And as for old Vealy getting the Dog to Moscow in time for the game," Gaffer said, returning to what they were all talking about before, "if you ask me – we ought to start weighing out that vodka right now."

10

TAFKAG was due to arrive at eight o'clock on Tuesday evening. He didn't often show up at the house. That would have meant him coming into contact with Luke's mum – and they both tried hard to avoid this. Which made good sense, really.

Luke's mum only had to look at TAFKAG's pink polka-dotted headbands and purple satin flares to start snorting. Everyone used to wear those sort of clothes back in the 1960s. Even Luke's mum (though she tried to deny it now). But it really wound her up to see a bloke *still* in hippie gear. And it wasn't as if he wore new versions of the old styles. This was the same kit he'd started wearing thirty years before (and hadn't washed quite as often since then as he should have).

But it wasn't just the clothes that got to Luke's mum. His whole attitude made her mad. Luke often wondered how his dad had ever had the nerve to ask her to marry him – or why she'd said yes. In all the years TAFKAG had spent trying to become a pop star, she kept on telling him to pack it in. (To be fair, so did a lot of record-company executives, *and* most of the punters at his gigs.) He didn't have the talent, she said. He didn't have the looks. He wasn't even young. And yet now after all the setbacks and heartbreaks, he'd finally managed to make his dream come true. Which just seemed to make her madder!

"What time did your dad say he'd be coming?" asked Rodney, looking anxiously at his watch for the umpteenth time that evening. It was 8:47 pm.

"Eight," Luke reminded him. "So he should get here just before nine."

"He could *never* get anywhere on time!" sighed Luke's mum. "It's just so inconsiderate. He thinks all we have to do is sit around here all evening." Which was, in fact, what she and Rodney did – almost every day of the week.

She glared at the muted TV screen as if she were about to hurl her glass of soluble aspirins right through it. She'd had a headache coming on ever since TAFKAG had said he was going to drop by.

The grandfather clock's big hand nudged upwards to mark another minute. Eight forty-eight. Then another. On the TV, a commercial break ended – so there was no chance of Luke's mum getting another glimpse of Desmond Lynam doing one of his gardening ads. She swooned over Des so much, she just blanked out the fact that he presented football matches for a living. And she *had* seen him once that evening, so her mood was really quite mellow now – compared to usual.

"It's no good," she declared, zapping off the TV, standing up and clutching her brow with her free hand. "My head is absolutely *killing* me. I've got to go upstairs and have a lie down."

"Ah ... now," gasped Rodney, springing up too and hopping about next to her. "Why don't you let me make you up a nice little bed on the sofa here? I'm sure Luke's dad will be here any minute, and he *did* so much want to talk to you."

She turned her steely glare on poor Rodders. "I need total darkness. Total quiet. Which I can't have down here. I'm going upstairs." And that's just what she did.

Almost before Luke and Rodney had time to look at each other, the doorbell rang: TAFKAG. It was as if he'd lost his nerve outside the house, then watched through the window until his ex-wife stomped off upstairs.

Rodney shook hands with him, and offered to take his big floppy hat with a yellow feather boa hanging off it. "Cheers but no, man," TAFKAG winked. "Think I'll keep the old thing on. Bit of protection if the going gets tough!"

"Well, Mum's not down here any more," Luke told him. "She got fed up waiting for you – and now she's up having one of her headaches."

"Yeah," TAFKAG sighed. "Bummer that I got held up. David Bowie called from the States with a party invite and, man, we had so much to catch up on!"

"So what are we going to do now?" Rodney asked. They were all still standing in the hall at the foot of the stairs. "I don't think she'll come down again."

"No I most certainly won't!" she yelled from her bedroom – and all three of the men in her life jumped. "Just ask him what he wants, will you, Rodney?"

"Er..." said Rodney, blinking away behind his glasses. Then he turned to TAFKAG, shrugged helplessly and said: "What was it that you – um – wanted?"

"Well hey," he called up the stairs. (He didn't have to shout – it wasn't a very big house.) "Whaddaya say to me zooming off to Russia with our first-born for three days next week?"

Luke gulped and stared at Rodney who was gulping too. Was that *it*? Was that the top and bottom of his cunning plan?

"Russia!" harrumphed his mum from her room. "In term time? It's obviously skipped your mind that Luke goes to *school*!"

"No, no," TAFKAG smiled back, but already he was panting. "I've OK'd it with the head. She thinks it would be a fab deal for him. Being there, hanging loose, getting the feel of the Russian street. Man, what an educational vibe! Just like he had in Munich. No, she's one hundred per cent in favour."

Luke and Rodney shivered. This wasn't great. TAFKAG frowned up the stairs as if he knew it too. And if this didn't work, Luke could forget about the second leg.

"And why *Russia*, for heaven's sake?" his mum yelled down.

TAFKAG swallowed and looked modest. "I'm pretty big over there right now. Sold out a big venue in Voronezh. And there's this other deal: it's so neat. This little town just outside Moscow – it's called Tafkag too! And the dudes on the council want to twin their town with *me*! Big civic event, banquet, the works."

"Don't be ridiculous!" Luke's mum stormed, saying what Luke and Rodney were thinking. As cunning plans went, this one could definitely be filed under "nutty". "You can't twin a town with a deadbeat singer-songwriter!"

"Hey, don't knock it," TAFKAG tried to protest, beads of sweat glistening all over his forehead under the hat. "I was voted fourth most interesting foreign recording artist in a St Petersburg magazine poll last month."

59

Luke shut his eyes. It was all over. Even if his mum had seen fifteen Des Lynam ads back-to-back to chill her out, no way was she going to fall for this. There was a better chance of Neil Veal getting the Dog to Moscow on time. The silence from upstairs told its own sorry story. She wouldn't even *answer*.

Then a miracle happened. She spoke.

"You wouldn't be going in that dreadful van of yours, would you?"

TAFKAG caught his breath. "Not a chance. Straight out of Heathrow. No messing."

Silence fell again. All three guys went up on tiptoe and clenched their fists – praying for her to give this seriously stupid suggestion the nod. That Des Lynam sighting must really have softened her up. Please! Please! *Please!*

"Well, if it's only for three days..." she said slowly.

Yes? *Yes?*

"Then, I suppose ... for the educational value ... all right."

That was typical of Luke's mum. You never knew where you were with her. Sometimes, Luke thought, she said the exact opposite of what you expected just to wind you up. (Maybe that's how she'd come to accept TAFKAG's marriage proposal?) But never in the history of shared childcare had one parent been so thrilled to get a result from the other. Neither had the child in question. And nor had his step-dad. The three of them flung their arms round each other and silently bounced up and down in the hall, mouthing "Yes. Yes. *Yeesssssss!*"

"What's going on down there?" Luke's mum asked as all the coats started to fall off their pegs because the hall was shaking so much.

"Nothing, dear," Rodney called up with a big breathless wink at the other two. *A town called Tafkag!* And she'd swallowed it! "Luke and his dad are just practising keeping warm for when they get to Russia!"

11

The next week was pretty dismal. Luke didn't see anyone from the club. Nor did he go near Ash Acre. Mostly he just slogged away at English, Maths, French, German, Physics, Chemistry, History, Geography, IT and Drama.

The headmistress said he had to work like stink to make up for the three school-days he was going to miss. "But don't wear yourself out studying," she warned him with an anxious look. "You're going to need all your wits about you over there in Moscow – and I don't just mean on the football pitch." Luke smiled and nodded, without knowing exactly what she *did* mean.

Albion had no game that Saturday, thanks to the postponement. So Benny's Boys could concentrate fully on the upcoming UEFA away leg. All Britain's other clubs had been knocked out already, so only little Albion were left to fly the flag now. That made them national heroes – at last.

Back in September, before the first round, the media hadn't given them a prayer of progressing in the competition. "Their British beef will not go down well on the continent," was the view of TV's Barry Venison. "But down they will go – probably by a hatful of goals." The *Sun* hadn't even wanted Albion to be allowed to take part. SPARE THE BLUSHES OF THESE NATIONWIDE NO-HOPERS! it had screamed. GIVE THEIR PLACE TO A PROPER TEAM FROM THE PREMIERSHIP!

You can imagine how pleased that made everyone feel at Ash Acre. It certainly made the players even keener to do well. But now, as they took a narrow but clear lead into the second leg of the quarter final, no one on the home front would say a bad word about them.

A huge pack of reporters was waiting at Heathrow when Luke and TAFKAG arrived for their flight on Tuesday afternoon. Most of the other players had also made their own way to the airport, and Benny's beard went even whiter with worry as he tried to round them all up. Some of the media-men helped him – and one found Casper and Keats wandering around lost in the wrong terminal. So when the whole squad was present and correct, the Big Bossman could hardly ignore the reporters' pleas for a quick press conference.

"Is there any chance at all of the Dog playing

on Thursday, Benny?" asked the man from the *Times*.

"He's on the road right now," Benny replied. "We've got our fingers crossed."

"But will he be match fit?" asked the guy from the *Mail*. "We hear he's spent the last three months tramping around in the mountains looking for sheep."

"That's all been part of a carefully-worked-out health and fitness programme," lied Benny. "I think you'll find him raring to go in Moscow."

"And if he delivers the goods over there," quipped Terry V, "we're thinking of putting some of the other lads on that fitness programme as well!"

"How about Jimbo Prince?" asked the woman from *PC Pro*. "Why isn't he travelling with you? Is it true that there's a major rift between you and him?"

"Mr Prince will be flying out in his own jet on Thursday," Benny smiled at her. "Before then, he's going for top-level remedial work on his injury at a Swiss clinic. As for a rift, we're both one hundred per cent behind each other."

"Mr Webb, Mr Webb!" cried an investigative reporter from Channel Four. "Lots of people have come a cropper in Russia over the years. Napoleon, Hitler, Cardiff City. Do you think your English game will travel well all the way to Russia?"

"Well, that's how the game got there in the first place," Benny smiled back. "From England. I've been reading all about it. It was these English mill-owner blokes who started up football over there, about a hundred years ago."

"But the game in Russia is very different now, isn't it?" the Channel Four guy went on, obviously wanting to make all the clever remarks himself. "Over the years it's been troubled with all kinds of problems. Violence, disasters. And you know all about the *dogovorni* phenomenon, I take it, Mr Webb?"

"Dog O'*What*?" asked Terry.

"*Dogovorni.* Match-fixing – when the score of a game is agreed in advance, so that people can bet on the result and make a pile of money."

"I dunno what you're on about," said Benny, narrowing his eyes. "The only thing *we*'ve agreed with Spartak Moscow is that we'll give them a rattling good game – and let the best team win on the night."

"Or rather, on the *nights*," Terry put in. "Since we're already halfway there."

"Quite so," said the Channel Four man. "But you *are* aware, aren't you, that the modern Russian game is closely linked to the world of serious crime?"

"Come again?" asked Benny.

"In 1997, for example, the director-general of the club you'll be playing on Thursday night was murdered in a country house outside Moscow." He blinked. "It can get pretty hairy out there."

Benny gulped. One or two of the players went a bit pale too – especially Dennis, whose eyes were out on stalks. "Well, I'm sure you've done your homework," Benny replied, "but my lads don't have anything to worry about. They're a thoroughly committed and highly disciplined bunch of professionals with only two things on their minds. One: to do their jobs to the best of their ability. And two: to represent not just English football but England itself on this wonderfully exciting occasion. Albion *is*, after all, what England was once called. And we at the club now regard ourselves as unofficial ambassadors – representing this great country of ours overseas in a proud and dignified way."

Before anyone could ask another question, a din of shrieks and hoots erupted from the magazine section of a nearby *John Menzies*. It really was quite deafening. Luke swivelled around to find the whole shop in uproar.

Right at the middle of the kerfuffle was Half-Fat. He was holding open a big glossy mag, high above his head, for half a dozen of the other players to squawk and whistle at. Meanwhile beside them, Chrissie and Madman were leaping up in a vain attempt to rip the thing out of Half-Fat's hands. And behind them four shop assistants were desperately trying to shut them all up.

"You've got to get a load of this, Boss!" Half-Fat roared across at Benny, waving the magazine. "It's Chrissie and Madman in the bath *together*!"

"And posing *in their Y-fronts* in the garden of their lovely home!" Craig bellowed, tears running down his cheeks as he fell about laughing.

"And wearing biker outfits to cook a fry-up..." Carl squealed helplessly, but he was cut off as several airport security officers rushed up and grabbed hold of all the proud and dignified ambassadors from Albion.

Luke realized what had happened. Half-Fat had found an early edition of *Alright, Mate!* – the men's mag which had recently done a photo shoot with Chrissie and the keeper. Unfortunately the security officers were going in a bit hard – and Narris and Half-Fat (to name just two of the players) weren't the sort to take stick without giving some back. Within moments, a full-scale ruck broke out. Newspaper stands went tumbling, shoppers were sent flying, a cash-till was knocked to the floor, several terrified women started screaming.

"Oh, stone me," Benny sighed as the reporters dashed away to get a closer, blow-by-blow look at the fight. "Still, it's good to get it out of their systems now, I suppose. It would be awful if that sort of thing happened in mid-air."

There were no casualties at the Battle of Heathrow *Menzies*.

It all blew over pretty fast when the security men realized who they were hitting. Then they started shaking the players' hands instead, asking them for autographs, and wishing them all the best in the chilly wastes of Russia. A crowd of passengers gathered too, to give them a grand send-off. But as they passed through customs, Luke heard one elderly gentleman mutter, "Carl Davey will have to go in a *lot* harder if they hope to get a result over there."

The staff on board the Russian *Aeroflot* plane couldn't have been nicer. Once they were airborne, Luke forgot all about the reporter's warnings about the land they were heading for. But he didn't know much about the place himself.

It was seriously big, that was for sure. Even so, Rodney had told him that for years it was just a part of the even bigger Soviet Union, along with the Ukraine, Georgia, Latvia, Lithuania and all sorts. This Soviet Union had been a "Communist" country, whatever that meant. But now, apparently, Russia was pretty much like everywhere else – except colder (minus eight degrees C when they'd left London, they'd all been told). Which explained why TAFKAG was now sitting next to his son in a manky Cossack hat and a filthy old ankle-length coat that looked as if it had been made out of distressed squirrel fur. Benny too, on Luke's other side, seemed to be wearing *two* sheepskin coats. But Russian planes were at least as warm as British ones, and within half an hour the smell coming off both older men put Luke right off his mile-high meal.

It wasn't a very long journey. In just over three hours they were touching down at Moscow's Sheremyetevo Two airport – and Dennis, deep in his tourist guidebook, was working himself into a major panic.

Now Dennis was different from most of the squad. He was actually *interested* in the places he travelled to with Albion. (Cool F was too, but he already seemed to have visited every country under the sun, so he took it all in his stride.) The rest of the guys could have been in Russia, Rochdale or the Rocky Mountains for all they cared – just as long as they could find a café that did beans on toast, a tacky shop for some souvenirs to take home, and maybe a bar to sample the local brew. (For weeks Craig had been practising the phrase *Dva piva, pazhalsyta* – Two beers, please. "Why two?" Gaffer had finally asked him at Heathrow. "Because I'm thirsty," Craig had replied.)

But Dennis liked to swot up on each place that Albion visited on their cup run. This was mainly because he was terrified of "abroad". Wherever he went, he liked to know in advance what kind of trouble to expect. "Hey," he said to Casper as they got up to leave the plane, "this place sounds *well* dodgy."

"We know, Dennis," Casper smiled. "You've bored us all rigid with your stories about Rasputin the Mad Monk and Ivan the Terrible and—"

"No, no," Dennis hissed, so hissily that four or five other players cocked an ear. "That's history. I'm talking about right now. *Today*." He waved his well-thumbed guidebook. "It's a right hotbed of villainy. Muggers, pickpockets, people who've just *bought* their driving licences. Everyone's trying to rip you off – especially the taxi-drivers. And then there's all these mafia types..."

"Nah," said Terry. "The mafia's in Italy. And America, of course."

"Don't you believe it," Dennis insisted. "They're here too. Loads of 'em. All running rackets and shooting one another up. Sounds like a nightmare."

"Oh, you'll be all right, Dennis, son," Benny grunted as he passed. "Just stick close to me and Tel and we'll get you home in one piece!"

But once they were off the plane – and feeling that subzero temperature even indoors – Luke thought the place *did* seem a bit worrying. He couldn't make head or tail of what anyone was saying around him. Policemen and soldiers were strutting about in all directions too. It was just as well the players had had their little punch-up at Heathrow, not here. They wouldn't have survived a single round with these guys.

"What's with all their signs, then?" Narris whispered to Ruel as they queued to have their passports and visas checked. He pointed at the strangely curly letters all around them. "Was the sign-writer drunk when he did them, or what?"

"Search me," shrugged Ruel. "You got any idea, Cool man?"

Frederick had his Walkman on and was reading a paperback novel, but he nodded. "Different alphabet. Cyrillic, they call it."

"Cyrillic?" said Narris. "Nice one."

Just then, there was a bit of argy-bargy at the desk up ahead. Benny craned his neck to see that Carl was being hauled out of the line. "Oh Lord," the Bossman gasped, "he hasn't tried to smuggle a pineapple into the country, has he? How many times have I got to tell 'im they've got laws about that sort of thing?"

But there was no fruit involved here. The difficulty seemed to have arisen from Carl's passport. Or, more specifically, from his passport *photo*. One armed man was now holding the offending picture up next to Carl's quivering face while another screwed up his eyes and looked closely from one to the other. Both of them were shaking their heads, and – weirdly – they were looking almost as frightened as their victim. "*Niet,*" said one. "*Niet!*" echoed the other. No. No!

"What seems to be the problem, officers?" Benny asked, striding forward. "Can I be of some assistance here. Oh, I *see...*"

Benny blinked at the small picture of his striker, swallowed, then looked hard at Carl. "Whatever were you *thinking* of, son?" he asked, horrified.

By now, everyone else in the Albion party had crowded around too. Luke couldn't get a very clear view from the back, but he could see what all the fuss was about. The picture must have been nearly ten years old. Carl would have been about eighteen, and it is so easy to make horrible mistakes at that age...

Nowadays Carl looked pretty normal. Wavy hair, square sort of face – nothing out of the ordinary. But as a younger man – oh my! From their awestruck silence, no one else in the squad knew about this stage in Carl's life either. And Carl probably wished he could forget all about it too.

For, in the flush of youth, he had shaved his head as smooth as Chrissie Pick's, yet left two fuzzy sideburns the size of great lamb-chops – and dyed them black. There was a vertical line of beard on his chin, dyed green. There was one dangly silver earring shaped like a skull. There was a safety pin through his left nostril... At that point, Luke had to look away. Enough was enough.

It didn't look good. On a poster for a film about a crazy serial killer, it might have looked OK. As an identikit photo of an alien mutant, it would have been fine. But in a *passport*? No way, Jose! Yet this *was* Carl Davey.

Taking a deep breath, Benny stepped up, covered the real Carl's hair with one hand and placed the other over his mouth. At once the guards saw that his eyes and nose were the same as in the photo. Slowly, shuddering, they began to nod. Snapping the passport shut, the first Russian stuffed it back into Carl's hand. The pained look on his face said: Don't *ever* do that to me again.

Carl heaved a sigh of relief as he was waved through the barrier. None of the stunned Albion players knew quite where to look. The next man up in the queue was TAFKAG. A bit timidly, the pop star handed over his passport. Oh no, thought Luke, fearing the worst. At certain stages of his career, the way TAFKAG had looked was probably a criminal offence over here.

The guard's eyes bulged, he put a hand to his brow, shook his head as if he might be about to throw up his dinner, then quickly he waved Luke's dad through. Enough was enough – even for him.

13

Night had fallen by the time Benny and the boys got out of the airport. It was almost light again before they all got into some taxis to take them to their hotel.

There wasn't any problem in *finding* taxis. It was just that the drivers seemed to want Andy Cole's weekly wage – in Russian roubles – to do the job. Benny did his best to haggle with them, but this wasn't easy since he didn't speak a word of Russian, nor did he really know how much a rouble was worth.

He kept on waving wads of 50,000-rouble notes, which seemed like a lot of money, but the drivers didn't want to know. Cool F eventually sorted it. Apparently this was old-currency money, and the drivers wanted the new sort. Frederick had brought enough of his own dosh to pay for everyone – but not till he'd haggled his way down to half the fares they'd wanted from Benny. And he did it all without saying a word – just by miming and hand gestures. "Eat your heart out, Mr Motivational Wilkie," murmured Casper as they climbed into the cars before speeding away through the empty night streets.

The airport was north-west of the city, but they were staying in *Komsomolskaya ploshchad* – Young Communists' Square – which was away to the north-east. It was too dark to see much of the area, but the hotel, a pocket-sized skyscraper, with a kind of church spire, was OK. The staff were friendly enough, and one or two of them even spoke English. Sort of.

Benny had put the players into pairs to share twin rooms. "That way, you can look out for each other," he explained when they'd collected their room keys. "And I want the *pairs* of you to look out for the *other* pairs too. Oh – and I want *no one* to leave this hotel without asking me first. Got that?"

"Got it, Boss!" they all agreed – Dennis more loudly than the rest. From the nervous way he was looking at the clerks and chambermaids, it seemed unlikely that he would ever leave his room, let alone the hotel.

Benny then unfolded a map of the city and held it up. "We're up here," he jabbed a finger at the north-east, "and the stadium is just round the corner – so there's no reason whatever for you to go *here*," he pointed at everywhere else.

"But what about all the famous sights in the

city centre, Boss?" moaned Craig. "The Kremlin and Red Square and everything? Playing chess in the park? I wanted to go and check all that out so I could put it in the novel."

Benny eyed him hard. "You're here to do a job of work, Craig. This isn't a flippin' holiday. And that goes for all the rest of you too. As far as I'm concerned, this is just like going to Plymouth or Barnet for a league game. You don't ever want to go nosing around *those* places, do you?"

"No, Boss!" chorused everyone except Chrissie, who said, "Well, *I* might. I used to go out with a really nice girl from Barnet." But Benny didn't hear. He'd noticed that Carl – over by the reception desk – wasn't paying attention any more. Instead he was deep in conversation with the desk clerk. "Carl!" he boomed. "Are you listening to me or what?"

Carl turned back to the group, grinning and rubbing his hands with glee. "Sorry, Boss. I was just making a little request. You said we weren't to leave the hotel – right? – so I've asked the staff to fetch something *in* for me."

"Oh no," sighed Narris, "not this week's *Beano*! They don't publish it over here, Carl. You'll just have to wait till you get home."

"No, no," laughed Carl. "A pineapple! I've got to have my pineapple for the game on Thursday." He nodded at the desk clerk, who gave him a big thumbs-up. "And Oleg here says he knows just where to get one. Problem solved!"

"Well, I'm thrilled for you," grunted Benny. "Now get up to your rooms and get a bit of kip, the lot of you. We're off to the stadium first thing for training."

Luke, who was in a special suite with Frederick *and* TAFKAG, slept like a top. In the morning he wasn't too sure about the breakfast of buckwheat pancakes and porridge with curd cheese and sour cream, but he ate it anyway and was very glad he did. Hardly anyone else joined him – preferring to stop their taxis for a pig-out at a McDonald's they spotted on the way to the stadium.

By daylight, this part of the city looked pretty grungy. The pavements were crowded with homeless drunks and old-age pensioners selling everything from shoelaces to packets of crisps. At every street corner there seemed to be a little market of some sort, but none of the goods on offer looked very tempting.

The stadium itself was quite impressive, though. A Spartak official who spoke a bit of English gave the visitors a quick guided tour before they got changed. You couldn't really help knowing it was called the *Lokomotiv* Stadium. Motifs related to trains kept popping up everywhere. "This is home stadium of old railway workers' team," the official told the squad. "Lokomotiv Moscow."

"But isn't Lokomotiv a completely different team from Spartak?" Dennis asked, immediately suspicious.

"*Da, da*," agreed the official. "But Spartak play here after crowd disaster in UEFA Cup tie at their own Luzhniki Stadium. Maybe 340 fans die. Terrible, terrible." He took a deep breath. "Now, till new 52,000-capacity Spartak stadium is built, Lokomotiv and Spartak share ground. You have same ground-share thing in England, I think. With your Wimbledog and Christmas Palace sharing Selfhurt Part?" The Albion party nodded, trying not to smile.

"Talking of Wimble*Dog*," Luke heard Gaffer ask Benny when they ran out on to the pitch later, "is there any news from the Bicycle Boys?"

"The Tandem Two?" growled Benny. "Not a thing. We'll just expect 'em when we see 'em. But if you want to get that vodka ready now, I won't stop you."

The boss put his lads through a tough two-hour session that blew all the cobwebs away. The ground was heavy but Luke found it easy enough to keep his feet in his trainers. It was weird to see all the touchline advertising boards in English, ready for the TV cameras the next night. *Tiger Beer, Yorkie, Teddy Smith Jeans* and *Burger King – Flame Grilling Tastes Better!*

That last one gave the less adventurous eaters an idea for a late lunch. On the way back to the hotel, most of them stopped off again for a taste of home. Just one taxi gave it a miss. Inside it were Luke, Frederick, Carl and Dennis. The young lads were keen to get back and try some beetroot soup followed by pork in a mushroom sauce. Carl just wanted to see if his pineapple had arrived. But Dennis had darker reasons for not going into the big burger joint.

"Didn't any of you notice?" he asked as they re-entered the hotel after Frederick had haggled the taxi fare right down. "Those two guys in long coats and furry hats? They were in the foyer here this morning. Then they were outside the stadium when we got there. And *then* at the burger place too."

"So what are you saying?" Carl asked. "They're trying to pluck up the courage to ask us for our autographs?"

Dennis scowled. "I don't like the look of them. They're tailing us. It's spooky."

"Ah, Mr Carl!" cried Oleg, the desk clerk, as Deadly Davey strolled in. "I have it for you! And at good price! Only one hundred roubles!" He reached down, then, almost before Carl or the others knew it, he tossed a small object their way.

It would have hit Carl smack in the face if Cool Frederick hadn't flicked a wrist and caught it. Raising one eyebrow, he offered it to the startled striker. "Enjoy," he said as the other two burst out laughing. "That's just cost you ten quid."

Carl put out a hand, took it and stared down sadly. A miniature tin of pineapple chunks in syrup! "Oh well," he sighed. "I guess my quest continues."

14

After lunch, Luke made a quick call home to tell his mum all about the make-believe village of Tafkag. She was more interested in telling *him* about a nasty-sounding new house with built-in garden gnomes that she'd just checked out.

Then Luke, Frederick and TAFKAG spent most of the rest of Wednesday watching TV in their suite. All six channels showed foreign films, so they watched *Spiceworld, Robin Hood Prince of Thieves* and two old James Bond movies. The only problem was that they all had Russian voiceovers.

TAFKAG, it turned out, fancied himself as a bit of a Russian speaker. He'd done a whole year of it at school and now, he said, it was all coming back to him. In the breaks between films, Luke heard him muttering away in Russian under his breath. Listening closer, he realized that it was the same few words again and again and again. "What *is* that you're saying?" he asked in the end.

TAFKAG turned to him, tilted back his headbanded head and proudly declared: " 'The grandmother works on the collective farm.' I remember it from my school textbook. I can write it out too – no messing, man. Hip sentence, eh?"

"I'm sure it'll come in really useful on this trip," grinned Luke.

"Oh yeah," TAFKAG nodded seriously. "I'm cool with the Russian lingo."

"Hey you guys," drawled Cool F, sounding almost excited. "Take a look."

He was pointing at the TV, where a news programme was now on. The reporter's words didn't mean a thing to Luke (or, Luke thought, to TAFKAG either – though he'd screwed up his face as if he was following every word).

For a few moments neither of them paid much attention to the figure bobbing about on a dusty country road behind the reporter's head, and in front of a very big crowd. Then they saw the blue and white hoops on his shirt. Then the mane of lank black hair. Then those glistening, enormously muscular thighs that came from a lifetime of pedalling around the Armenian mountains. It was the Dog! But what was he *doing*?

"He's playing keepy-uppy!" gasped Luke. "Look: the counter at the bottom of the screen shows his score! Four thousand and two, four thousand and three..."

"And look," TAFKAG added, "that other little table shows how many he's done in other places along the way! Hey *man* – twelve thousand five hundred and forty seven in Rostov..."

"And ten thousand nine hundred and seventeen in Kharkov," breathed Luke.

"Which means he's still miles from here," Cool F pointed out.

"But why d'you think he's doing it?" TAFKAG asked.

At that point, as if in answer to the question, the camera cut away from Dog and the crowd to a roadside table. Behind it sat a tall, thin bloke in a luminous green Lycra one-piece, Raybans and a cycling helmet. Vealo!

"He's taking money from all those punters!" cried Luke.

"They must have laid bets that the Dog wouldn't get past a certain score," suggested TAFKAG. "Vealy must be really cleaning up there."

Cool Frederick nodded. "Nice scam," he purred, his feet nestling in the *Fredator* trainers that Nifty Neil had got Adidas to make for him.

"I don't think we should tell Benny about it, though," suggested Luke. And both the others nodded firmly in agreement. "I only hope he wasn't watching this station himself."

"No way, man," smiled TAFKAG. "If he had

been, we'd have heard the dude's roars in *here*!" He switched off the set. "Now Fred," he said, reaching out for his guitar, "how's about you and me getting down for a jam session? I've got a few new tunes I'd like to lay on you."

Luke took that as a cue to get out of the room as fast as possible. The early versions of his dad's songs could be pretty hard on the ear. Some of the finished versions weren't a whole lot easier. "I think I'll go and see if any of the others are down in the lounge," he said, slipping out quickly.

The ground floor was dimly lit. At first glance, it seemed to be deserted. Then Luke heard a voice over by the reception desk. Carl's. And from the shapes he was making with his hands, he was trying to explain to the puzzled-looking girl that he wanted a real pineapple.

Finally Carl gave up and stalked over to Luke. "It's no good," he said, shaking his head. "There's a major shortage of pineapples in the city. I even nipped out earlier to the shops and markets when Benny wasn't looking, but you can't get one for love nor money. And I so *need* a pineapple! I haven't got a cat's chance of scoring unless Craig gives me a hit."

Luke shrugged sympathetically. But out of the corner of his eye, he saw a man in a long coat step up to the desk from the shadows. He bent forward to talk to the receptionist, she pointed at Carl, then he turned and came over, smiling.

Stopping very close in front of Carl, he tugged his furry hat a bit lower, then said in a deep whisper, "You want to meet ... *Pineapple People*?"

"I'm sorry?" said Carl, stepping back a pace, partly because the stink of vodka on the man's breath was so strong. "What did you say?"

The man stepped forward. "You want to see..." he winked, and maybe hiccuped too, "*Pineapple ... People*?"

"Well I do need a pineapple, yes," stammered Carl. "*Are* there people who sell them here in Moscow? I've been trying to get one for ages, but..."

"We get you *fifty thousand* pineapples," the man slurred. "You understand?"

"Really?" Carl's eyes popped. "Oh, well, that really would be—"

"All settled then," the man cut him off. "Room number?"

"My room number?" said Carl. "Well, it's 132. Why, do you think you can...?"

"You will be given instructions. For tomorrow." Again he winked, and this time he definitely burped. "I arrange meeting with ... *Pineapple People*." With a creepy leer, he turned on his heel, then swayed away through the hotel doors. Out on the street, another man in similar clothes was waiting. They both got into the back of an extremely smart-looking limousine and ghosted off.

Carl looked surprised but hopeful too. "He seemed like a nice enough chap," he said. "And he really sounded quite confident about the pineapple."

"Umm," said Luke, staring at the space which the limousine had left in the street. He didn't say a word to Carl, but those two guys looked *just* like the ones that Dennis had been talking about after training.

They're tailing us, Dennis had said. Was Luke getting paranoid now too? Maybe so. But suddenly he was wondering if Dennis might just be right...

15

Benny put the squad through a gentle session the next morning. He didn't want to wear anyone out on the day of the big game. But after they'd showered and changed it was still only 1:00 pm and the match didn't start until 9:00. In one sense that was good: there was still time for Vealy to deliver the Dog. But it did leave the rest of the squad with rather too much scope to get into mischief.

"Now I want you to look after yourselves properly over the next eight hours," Benny told them with his most solemn face. "No stupid muckin' about." He looked into the eyes of each player in turn. "I think you all know the score."

"Yeah, Boss," chirped Chrissie. "It's two-one to us right now. Or does that mean it's three-two to the Russkies, Carl? Away goals *do* count double. Don't they?"

Everyone looked at Carl and laughed. All through the cup-run he'd struggled to under-stand the away-goals rule. However many times his team-mates tried to explain that an away goal counted double only if the aggregate scores from *both* legs were level, he couldn't seem to get it. Against Bayern in Germany, he'd even wondered if he had to score just one and a half times to bag a hat-trick.

"You know what I'm talking about," Benny went on. "I want you all to do *nothing* between now and the kick-off except focus on football. Got that? Chill out at the hotel, *think* your way right through the game ahead. That's what Terry, me and Ruel are gonna be doing. And like I said before – look out for each other. If anyone looks like going off the rails, get him sorted! Right?"

"Right, Boss," said Gaffer with a captain's salute. "Maybe a few of us could get together and talk Carl through the away-goals rule."

"Good idea," agreed Half-Fat. "That ought to take about eight hours!"

"Just shut it, you lot," Carl muttered, but his mind seemed to be on something else. And Luke had a pretty fair idea what. So, in the taxi back to the hotel, which he shared with Carl, TAFKAG, Cool Frederick and Dennis, he brought it up.

"Hey," he asked, "have those guys from last night been in touch again?"

Carl glanced at the other three before answering. "Well ... yes, as it happens."

"What guys?" asked Dennis, and Luke quickly filled him in on the "Pineapple People".

"That sounds *well* dodgy to me," breathed Dennis, wrinkling his brow. "I *knew* those blokes were on our tails. How much did they want for their stupid pineapple, Carl? An arm and a leg, I bet."

"Actually," said Carl, "I haven't *got* the pineapple – not as yet."

"They wanted a down-payment first, right?" asked TAFKAG. "Dosh up front?"

Carl squirmed in his seat. "No, actually. They didn't mention money. It was all very quick. They just told me to be in the hotel foyer at seven this evening."

"Perhaps they're going to make a major presentation?" suggested Luke. "Invite the media along and everything? The official match-pineapple handover."

"Search me," shrugged Carl. "But I've just gotta get one for tonight. And look, guys, don't mention this to Benny, OK?"

"Why not?" asked Dennis, looking more alarmed by the moment. "You're not going to be leaving the hotel or anything, are you?"

"No..." said Carl after a pause. "No ... I'm not."

And then he changed the subject to Casper's mild groin-strain in training. But Luke knew that something was up. There was more to this seven o'clock deal than Carl was letting on. And all afternoon, back up in his hotel room, he got more and more bothered about it. Until finally, at 6:55 pm, he stopped trying to write a history essay on the Reasons for Hitler's Rise to Power, and stepped across to the door.

"I'm just going down to the foyer," he called out to TAFKAG, who was strumming an acoustic guitar in the bathroom.

"Oh, is it time for the pineapple drop?" cried his dad. "Count me in as well."

When they got to the ground floor, they found Frederick in a big armchair, flipping his mobile phone shut. "Here to check out Carl?" he asked. "Me too."

"And us," said a voice behind them. They turned to see a determined Dennis coming down the stairs. (He never took lifts – in case they got stuck between floors.) And behind him were Madman, Chrissie, Narris and Craig.

"It's nice to have a bit of excitement," grinned Madman. "Till Dennis told us about this, we were all going nutty with boredom up there!"

"Or nuttier than ever, in your case," said Narris. "But look, is that Carl's contact?" He pointed at one of the guys from the night before, who was hopping from foot to foot in the doorway, glancing repeatedly at his watch and – very clearly – *not* carrying a pineapple.

At that moment, another lift arrived and Carl

stepped out, wearing a long leather coat. Not noticing the other players, he took one look at his contact and strode across towards him. *Focus on football*, Benny had instructed them. You could forget that with Carl. At this point in time, he was focused purely on fruit.

He leaned in close to the man in the furry hat. Briefly they exchanged a few words. Then, without a backward glance, Carl accompanied him into the street.

That was too much for Dennis. "We've got to stop him!" he cried. "Benny said not to leave the hotel. There's no telling *where* he might end up!"

"Come on!" answered Craig, waving to the others as he set off across the foyer. "And all this for a flippin' pineapple. Carl needs his head examined!"

Luke, TAFKAG, Cool F, Narris, Chrissie, Madman and Dennis gave chase. And just then Half-Fat wandered out of the lounge reading a week-old copy of the *Sun*. With a puzzled look, he tagged along too.

But when they got out on to the seriously cold, lamplit street, they all gaped in amazement. Carl was doing something that the Dog would *never* have done: he was climbing into a form of powered transport. But it wasn't a car, nor was it a taxi, nor even a limousine like the night before.

No. With a bit of help from the man in the

furry hat, Carl "What's the Score?" Davey was swinging his way up into the cab of an enormous lorry – an old-fashioned, camouflaged ex-army troop-carrier!

16

"Halt!" yelled Dennis, slipping straight into military jargon. He held up a hand and Furry Hat turned in surprise to face him.

"It's OK, Dennis," Carl called down anxiously from the cab. "I'll only be a few minutes. I'm just going to see some men about a pineapple."

"You're not going *anywhere*!" Dennis growled.

"Not without us, anyway," grinned Madman – who obviously wasn't keen to go back and be bored again in the hotel.

Furry Hat gulped and blinked. "You *all* come?" he asked, astonished. At that, the driver started up the great vehicle's thunderous engine, and Furry Hat suddenly hoisted himself up next to Carl. Dennis grabbed hold of the door.

"Where are you taking him?" he shouted. "What's going on? *Tell* me!"

"Sssshh, Den!" hissed Carl. "Benny might hear! Then I've *really* had it."

"Get down from there at once!" Dennis said

in a lower voice. "You've got no idea who these people could be! They could take you anywhere! And we've all got to meet Benny in the foyer in half an hour to leave for the stadium."

"Hey!" Furry Hat cut in. "Rest of you coming, or what? If yes – get in back!"

An odd moment followed. The Albion Nine all looked at one another. At once Dennis began to shake his head, but it was Chrissie who spoke.

"Well look," he said, "Benny's told us to look out for each other. And Carl's not coming out. So there's only one way: *we'd* better go with *him*."

"You must be..." Dennis cried, but before he could gasp the words "out of your mind", the other eight all scuttled to the back of the truck and began diving up and into the darkness under the fabric covering. And, in the spirit of if-you-can't-beat-them-join-them, Dennis finally scrambled on board himself, just as the driver got his great juggernaut going.

No one said much for the first few minutes. They had to concentrate pretty hard on not rolling all over the place. There was nothing in the back to cling on to, and the driver took corners about as smoothly as Luke's mum when she'd heard they were doing a special offer on hyacinth bulbs at the garden centre.

Luke guessed that everyone was thinking the

same thing: that they were cutting this a bit fine. It was getting on for 7:20 now, and Benny had asked them all to assemble at 7:30. If they weren't back on time, he'd go absolutely ape. And all this, as Craig had pointed out, for the sake of one measly pineapple.

"We seem to be leaving the bright lights behind," Chrissie said, breaking a long, increasingly shivery silence. It was true. As the lorry rattled on along straighter roads now, they could see only stars out of the back, not street lights.

"Bit of a magical mystery tour, eh?" asked TAFKAG.

"They're taking us right out into the country," murmured Dennis, quaking. And Luke then *knew* what was passing through some of their minds: what that Channel Four reporter at Heathrow had said – about Spartak's director-general being murdered in a country house just outside the city. *It can get pretty hairy out there*, he'd warned them. Luke shivered, and not just from the cold.

The lorry must have been doing almost eighty now. But the journey still lasted for another ten minutes. By that stage, half the Albion lads were feeling dreadfully car-sick as well as bitterly cold and worried to death. And the last part was the worst of all. Suddenly they swung off the road and, without losing much speed, they seemed to be bumping and bouncing straight across a field.

While Dennis and Madman retched, Luke and TAFKAG banged hard on the back of the cab to try to get the driver to slow down. It did no good. But then, as abruptly as Paul Ince loses his rag, they juddered to a halt.

There were still no lights outside. There were dogs, though. Lots of them from the sound of it. And could they bark and howl! Half-Fat looked across at Craig and rolled his eyes. "Benny will be making a noise like that now," he said. "He'll be doing his nut in that foyer." Once again Luke lit up his watch-face and glanced at the time. Seven forty. Just eighty minutes to kick-off.

"Oh, what have we *done*? What have we *done*?" whimpered Dennis, head in hands.

"We've come to get a pineapple!" said a bright voice at the truck's open end. It was Carl, down from the cab, flanked by two men who just about had their leaping Alsation dogs under control. "Are you lot coming inside?"

"Inside?" asked Craig. "You mean we're not out in the middle of nowhere?"

"No, no – we've pulled up in front of a big country house! Smashing place."

Just as he said that, a guard in battle dress marched into view and peered in at the large group of visitors from England. He had a very large machine gun.

"Oh *nooooo*!" moaned Dennis. "I'm not moving from here. Not one inch!"

"Me neither," chorused Madman, Chrissie, Craig and (surprisingly for a soccer hard-man) Narris.

"Hey, let's just do this thing," said Frederick, jumping out. "We've got a game to get to." Half-Fat went next – then TAFKAG. So Luke leapt down too.

"Hey!" grinned the goon with the gun. "Studless Sensation! Maybe you autograph my bullet-belt later? For my daughter – you know? She big fan."

"Oh *look*!" purred Carl, pointing to the grand entrance of a palace-like house.

Under a dazzling security light, a short balding man in a suit and shades was beckoning to them. This was plainly the guy they had come all this way to see. Five or six other goons in suits stood behind him, crunching their knuckles. And although he was about a foot shorter than them, *he* was Mr Big. He was the one who called the shots here, the one who had what Carl wanted.

For while in one hand he held a big Cuban cigar, in the other he was proudly holding up for all to see ... a pineapple!

Carl lurched forward at once – still a bit shaky on his legs after the bumpy ride. He pulled a wad of Russian banknotes out of his pocket and offered them to little Mr Big. "Name your price!" cried the excited and much-relieved striker. "I know how precious these things are in Russia! Just say how much!"

Mr Big simply laughed, turned on his heel and beckoned to Carl to follow him into the mansion. Luke, Frederick, TAFKAG and Half-Fat set off in pursuit. But as they made to go inside too, the half-dozen heavies strung themselves out across their path, blocking them off. "*Niet,*" said the middle one, waving his hand. None of the Albion lads tried to argue. These guys were *well* tooled up – the bulges under their suits were clear even after the security light went out.

"You speak Russian, don't you, TAFKAG?" said Half-Fat. "Ask 'em what's going on here. And tell 'em we're in a hurry."

TAFKAG cleared his throat and was probably going to give them *The grandmother works on the collective farm* till Luke elbowed him into keeping quiet. As the dogs kept barking all round, Luke thrust his hands deep into his puffer jacket pockets. "So what do we do now?" he said to the other three.

Half-Fat shrugged. "What *can* we do? Just wait here for Carl to do his deal, then scarper? Although knowing Carl and maths, he'll probably end up paying half his year's wages for the stupid thing. Nice business for these guys."

"Yes, but what kind of business *is* it?" asked Luke. "This seems like an awful lot of trouble just to buy one pineapple."

"These guys don't deal in ones," Cool Frederick said softly, nodding beyond the mansion. Luke looked and saw several enormous warehouses, guarded by militiamen toting pump-action shot-guns. Even as they watched, another lorry pulled up in front of the nearest. At once a gang of lifters, wearing what looked like space-suits, dashed out to start the unloading.

"Wow!" gasped TAFKAG. "Now *that* looks like serious stuff. Radioactive?"

"Nuclear?" suggested Frederick.

"Is this a *bomb* factory?" gaped Half-Fat.

Frederick nodded slowly. "It could be. Among other things." He breathed in. "I'm starting to suss this now. That namecheck – the Pineapple People. I *knew* I'd heard it before..." He raised his shades to look hard at the line of heavies.

The one who'd said *Niet* smirked back.

"Tonight," he said, in such a heavy Russian accent that the words seemed to crash to the ground beneath him and make it shake, "English lose." To show what he meant, he made a brief kicking motion with one foot. "Eh?"

"Ah well," Half-Fat replied, "it's a funny old game, football. Never over till the fat lady sings and all that. It can always go either way – that's the beauty of it."

The goon's face darkened. "*Niet!*" he rumbled. "English lose. *Da?*" Then he made a more confusing gesture – as if he was fingering money. And after that, he titled back his head, maybe to indicate what was now going on in the house.

"Sorry mate," said Half-Fat, shrugging. "Don't understand. *Nil comprendo.*"

The other goons chuckled, and one said something in Russian. Luke, of course, didn't know what any of it meant. But one word was familiar. *Dogovorni.* He knew he'd heard it before, but he couldn't remember for the life of him where. Frederick, however, was nodding quite fast now. He was swallowing hard too. "What is it?" Luke asked. "What's happening here?"

"I think we'd better ask *him*," Cool F

suggested, as Carl reappeared, still accompanied by little Mr Big and his pineapple.

The line of heavies parted to let Carl through. Before he did so, Mr Big shook his hand and ceremonially presented him with the prize piece of fruit. Carl grinned broadly, thanked him, and trotted back up to his four mates. "OK guys," he beamed. "*Now* we're in business! Let's go play football!"

There was, indeed, no time to lose. The five of them leapt back up into the lorry, where the others were still huddled up like frightened hostages. "D-d-don't sit *anywhere* near us!" Narris warned Carl in a groggy, petrified voice. "Y-y-you'll pay for all this later, I can promise you..."

As soon as they were on board, the driver got going – but not before one more person scrambled up to join them for the return journey. Luke blinked. It was the guard who had earlier asked for his autograph. Only now he'd changed from his combat clothes into red-and-white Spartak supporters' togs.

"I hitch lift with you!" he laughed. "*Come on you Spartaks!* – eh? We definitely win tonight now. Go through to semis, *da*?" He winked at Carl, who smiled back from the corner where he sat apart with Luke and Frederick.

They were bumping back across the field now – and already Narris, Dennis and a couple of the others were shivering, groaning and clutching their stomachs. Carl, however, seemed as happy as a sandboy.

"So how much did you have to pay in the end?" Luke asked Carl.

Carl shrugged. "Nothing, as it happens. We hardly talked about fruit. He said this was just a "taster" – so he must've thought I wanted to eat it. I think he might just have given it to me, actually. It was hard to understand *what* he was saying, to be honest. Most of the talk was about football. Tonight's game. He was a bit of a fan."

"He said we'd lose, right?" murmured Frederick, out of earshot of the others, whose teeth were all chattering so much, they probably wouldn't have heard anyway.

"Well, yeah. He did keep saying that. *Two-nil, two-nil*, he kept saying. *Two-nil half-time, two-nil full*. It seemed pretty important to him. Passionate about his team, I guess. In the end, I just said 'Well, you're probably right, mate'. I had to – so's I could get us all away to the game."

"You agreed that Albion would lose two-nil?" Frederick repeated in a flat whisper.

"Well – just to shut him up," Carl hissed, "and so I could get out of there..."

"And he shook your hand right after you said it?"

"Well – yes – as it happens. Why?"

Frederick let a long, slow sigh escape. A guy

as cool as Frederick could never look *worried*, but this was the closest that Luke had ever seen him get to it.

"Oh, no reason" he breathed, eyeing the off-duty guard. But when he looked at Luke he closed his eyes tight for a moment.

"Hey F-Fred," Craig called out then, slapping himself for warmth, "you got your m-m-mobile? Why not give Benny a bell at the hotel? Tell him we're on our way?"

"Oh wow," said Madman, "he'll be having k-kittens in that foyer by now."

"Full-grown w-wildcats, more like," Chrissie corrected him. "Lions, l-leopards, s-s-s-sabre-toothed tigers..."

Cool F tried the hotel switchboard but got no reply.

"They m-must all be watching the pre-match build-up on TV," suggested Half-Fat. "Oh, what sort of a s-s-state is the boss going to be in?"

"Let's just hope the D-Dog has arrived," groaned Dennis. "That might take his mind off the rest of us for a bit." He glared at Carl. "What a *mess* this all is! First Dog, now you. W-w-wouldn't the world be a far, far better place without s-s-stupid s-s-strikers!"

18

The truck roared on through the night. Luke knew from Frederick's expression that something bad was up. Something he couldn't talk about in front of the others. And that word *dogovorni* kept eating at him. Where *had* he heard it before?

For the time being though, they all had yet another problem to fret about. At the outskirts of the city they hit the mother of all traffic jams. Every car in Moscow seemed to be going to the match. But at the rate they were moving, it looked like the match would have only one team playing in it.

"We'll never get there," moaned Chrissie. "We won't reach the h-h-hotel by nine, let alone the stadium."

"And Benny will be f-foaming at the mouth by now," Craig agreed. "Can't you give him another try on your mobile, Frederick?"

Cool Frederick tried for maybe the tenth time to dial up the hotel. Again no one answered.

"Maybe all the staff have g-g-gone to the game?" suggested Half-Fat.

"Well hey, look," said TAFKAG, "why d-d-don't we get the driver to head straight for the stadium? That would save us a bit of time, right?"

"Good think!" cried the guard. "I go tell." And he leapt down from the almost stationary truck, re-routed the driver and came back at once, all smiles. "Should be no problem. We get to Lokomotiv Stadium in ten minutes. *Then* Spartak beat you! Two goals to nil!" He made the money-fingering gesture and nodded at Carl. "And *you* get *your* reward, hmm? Fifty thousand? Very nice!"

Fifty thousand? The players who could hear him stared back blankly. Luke glanced at Cool F who had lifted his shades and was pinching the top of his nose. But no one spoke for the next ten minutes as the truck lurched and hiccuped along ever closer to Albion's date with destiny.

It was touch and go whether most of the passengers *could* have spoken. Even TAFKAG was looking pretty green around the gills now, and he'd had a lifetime's experience of jerky driving – his own. But finally the guard told them they had arrived. Well, almost.

"We travel rest of way quicker on feet," he cried, jumping down and beckoning to the others to follow. That was easier said than done. Only Luke, Frederick and Carl were at all steady on their feet now. But when everyone was safely on the street, they started to fight their way through the crowds, led by the guard.

He didn't care who he knocked over in clearing a path. As the stadium came into view, the players and TAFKAG didn't have to push and shove very much for themselves. Carl, holding his pineapple like a rugby ball, was at the head of the Albion pack. Just behind him came Luke and Frederick, who was still trying to get through to Benny on his mobile.

"He must have left for the stadium now, any-way," panted Luke, glancing at his watch. "There's less than half an hour to kick-off. But look: tell me. What's happened? What did Carl agree to back there? What's he dropped himself in?"

Frederick jogged closer to his mate. Then he checked that no one else from Albion was close enough to overhear. "*Pineapple People* – right? Code-name. They're a mafia gang. Big-time mobsters. I read about them back home. Arms deals, money laundering, black-marketing..." he lowered his voice. "Match fixing."

Match-fixing! That was what *dogovorni* meant. Guys betting mega amounts of money on football match results – then making sure the results went *just* the way they wanted.

"Oh no," murmured Luke, remembering

two-nil, two-nil and *fifty thousand – very nice.*
"You mean they've bribed Carl to throw the game?"

"Well, they probably *think* they have – but Carl's well in the dark about it."

"No change there, then." Luke watched Carl ducking and weaving his way through the fans up ahead. "But do you think we should tell him?"

"No way!" snorted Cool F. "That would put him right off his game."

"Ye-e-s," said Luke hesitantly. "But what will happen if we *don't* lose two-nil? And besides, Carl's only one player. How's he supposed to get Albion to lose all on his own?"

Frederick shrugged as they slowed down near the ground's main entrance. "They think he'll work on the rest of us, I guess. Then give us some of his winnings."

Fifty thousand, Luke remembered. Fifty thousand what, though? Pounds, roubles? "And if we don't go down two-nil," he said slowly, "these Pineapple People won't be very happy about that, will they?"

Coming to a standstill, Frederick turned to face him. But before he could say a word, the guard came up and clapped a mighty hand on both their shoulders. "I leave you here," he boomed over the din of the queuing fans. "Pineapple People very pleased to do business with Albion team. Just remember – two-nil at half-time, two-nil at full. Then everybody happy!"

"Look," Luke began in a faint voice, "I think there's been a terrible mistake..."

The guard's hand tightened on his shoulder. "*Niet*. No mistake. Understand?"

"Yes, but..." Luke tried to argue – but then the guard's grip became so tight, he thought his shoulderblade might snap.

"No, Studless," he said. "Pineapple People don't like mistakes. Understand?"

"Yes!" winced Luke. "Yes – absolutely. I understand!"

"Is good! I go watch now. Have good game." He winked. "May best team win!"

Luke, rubbing his shoulder, and Frederick looked at each other as he strode off. The rest of the Albion players and TAFKAG were straggling up to them now – all looking horribly unprepared for a major European tie. Carl, meanwhile, was waiting up ahead of them by the stadium's main, graffiti-covered entrance.

Luke heard him call: "Come on, you lot – chop-chop! We've only got fifteen minutes to get changed... *AAAAAARGGGGHHHH!*"

Luke swivelled round just in time to see the pineapple go flying into the air, while Carl keeled over as if he'd just been stabbed in the back.

19

Carl hadn't been stabbed from behind. He'd been whacked, hard, on the back of the head with a single shinpad. At once half-a-dozen armed policemen raced over. But when they saw what had happened, they backed off again – rolling their eyes and tut-tutting in a "What-Do-You-Expect-From-The-English?" way.

For Carl's attacker wasn't a Moscow mugger. Nor was he a hungry Russkie desperate for a rare taste of pineapple. He was, in fact, some-one who really didn't hit footballers at all as a rule – even if at times he badly *wanted* to hit them, just to knock some sense into their flippin' thick skulls.

"Benny!" gasped all the Albion players who were not too truck-sick to talk.

"Cor, steady on, Boss," sighed Carl, twisting around in a daze, snatching up his pineapple from the ground and looking at the seriously shirty Supremo in double Sheepskin. But *under* the two hairy coats, was that an Albion kit on

Benny? It was! "Are you playing then, Boss?" asked Carl.

"I thought I was gonna have to!" fumed Big Benny. "We was struggling to make up the numbers, what with you lot bunkin' off like that! Where have you *been*? No, on second thoughts, I don't wanna know. I don't think my poor old heart can take any more shocks. Nor can Terry and Ruel. I've got *them* on standby in there as well! Not to mention young Jimbo!"

"*Jimbo?*" cried the players in despair. "He's h-h-here?"

Benny's face seemed to crumple. "He's here and he's made a miracle recovery at that Swiss clinic. He's not up for a full ninety minutes, he reckons, but he's put himself on the bench – and he's told me he's *gotta* come on at some stage. We've just got to lump it. There's not a thing that any of us can do."

The players looked at one another, dumbstruck. That was that, then. With Jimbo on the pitch they didn't have a prayer, no matter how often Craig hurled that pineapple at Carl's bottom. After all their other troubles – now *this*!

Some Spartak fans had come to help Carl to his feet (and gaze in wonder at his pineapple). A crowd of others pressed in on Luke and Frederick, begging for autographs. But Benny wasn't having any of that. "Come on, my lot –

inside! All of you! You've hardly got time to get changed before we get started!"

The boss stood aside, and smacked each player on the side of the head as they passed. No one complained. They all knew Benny was simply showing his relief; there wasn't any malice in it. Luke and Frederick were the last in, after signing just a few autographs. Benny didn't lay a finger on them.

"I was most worried about you two," he admitted, shaking his great shaggy head. "At the end of the day, you're only kids, after all – even if we *do* depend on you like we've never done before to get a result here tonight."

"We're OK, Boss," Luke assured him. "Let's just focus on the football now."

"Good idea," said Benny, following them inside and down to the Away Team dressing-room. "And I'd better change out of this kit before I get arrested for impersonating a soccer player."

But as Luke slipped into his shirt, shorts and socks, he found it pretty hard to focus on football himself. Partly because Jimbo gave everyone an absolute earful about showing up so late. Then he made them all sit through a "rousing" medley of old *Eurovision Song Contest* intros on the ghetto-blaster. But mainly Luke's thoughts were still full of the Pineapple People.

It was all so complicated. But there was sure to be trouble – either way.

If by some fluke they *did* go down two-nil tonight – and news ever got out about Carl's "deal" – then every Albion player would be banned for life. Yet if Benny's Boys got some other result, the Pineapple People were hardly likely to say, "Oh well, that's life. We're sure you gave it your best shot". They would be *extremely* unhappy with Carl and the rest of them. They would also be a good deal poorer after losing all the money they had bet on Spartak winning two-nil. They would feel let down. And Luke sensed that they would want to show this. In a physical way. With more than just a tap on the head with a shinpad...

"*AAAARRRRRGGHHHHHH!!!!!*"

Luke almost jumped out of skin as an unearthly roar rang round the dressing room. When the dust settled, he saw Carl blissfully rubbing his bottom, where Craig had just given him an industrial-strength hit with the pineapple.

"That ought to do the trick!" the striker grimaced through his pain.

"It had *better*," groaned Half-Fat, "after all the fuss we had about getting it."

Several of the others nodded grimly. But Luke could see how groggy they still looked. That truck ride really had taken it out of them. And, in Dennis' case at least, it hadn't helped to be scared stiff for so long. Only supersub Jimbo looked really fired up for the battle ahead. So fired up that when Benny called for some hush for his team-talk, JP leapt up instead and yelled:

"We're here to do a job of work! We're here to prove to the world that English football still rules! We're here to fight and die for the name of Castle Albion FC! So just remember when you wear those blue-and-white hoops with pride out there tonight: *Nobody ever* BEATS *the Albion – they just score more goals!*"

You could have heard a pin drop as his last high-pitched words sank in. Not one person in the room knew what he was talking about. But everyone started to nod, just to keep him happy.

"I think they've got the message, Benny," Jimbo called across to the gaping manager. "They know what this is all about tonight. And they know that they can get the result we need without the help of any Armenian pedal-pusher!"

The Dog! In all the excitement, Luke had completely forgotten about the Sharp Shooting Shepherd's race against time to get to the game.

"He didn't make it, then?" asked Chrissie glumly. "Does that mean Vealo…"

"…will have to drink his own weight in vodka?" asked Terry V with a flashing grin. "Yes, I'm afraid it does. I've already put in my order to the off-licence."

"I'm saving a place for him on the bench, though," sighed Benny. "Just in case..."

"But don't even think about Vealy or the Dog now," Terry went on. "You've got a tie to go out and wrap up. You did all the hard work when you beat this lot in England. All you gotta do here is get a draw. *Just go and do it!*"

20

All they had to do was draw. Nil-nil, one-one, two-two. Any level score would have suited the visitors. Add that on to the two-one scoreline from Ash Acre – and through little Albion would go to the semi-final of the UEFA Cup.

Luke knew all this as well as anyone. (And a lot better than Carl, who was still deep in the dark when it came to aggregate scores.) But during the kick-in, he seriously doubted that CAFC could do it. So many of the lads looked so *dazed*.

When Madman trotted behind the goal to fetch a horribly wayward shot from Narris, he seemed to wobble all over the place. Chrissie, too, was taking three swings before connecting with the ball every time he tried a short pass to Gaffer. As for Dennis, he squatted down to pant hard and get his bearings – and that was just after shaking hands with his opposite number in a Spartak shirt.

It didn't look promising. And Albion's

marvellously loyal travelling supporters had spotted trouble too. There must have been two thousand of them in the stadium – swigging back Spartak's own-brand Cola and tucking into cones of sunflower seeds. And although they were heavily outnumbered, they must have been giving the rows of soldiers in front of them earache from all their singing.

"Madman, Madman, give us a wave!" they bellowed, led by that unmistakable one-man thunderstorm, Rocky Mitford. But when Madman dizzily turned and waved at some people in the opposite stand, they chanted even louder:

"We're over HERE, you prannet!"

Then they noticed something odd about Keatsy. Two thousand fingers pointed his way as the brand new cry arose:

"Shirt on the wrong way! You've got your shirt on the wrong way!"

And he had! The big red number ten was on his chest! But seeing the problem was easy. Solving it was altogether more difficult. As the young striker staggered about, tugging the shirt up over his head, he got it caught round his ears, jerked too hard, lost his balance, and fell in a heap near the penalty spot.

Not good. Luke winced at Frederick, who raised an eyebrow back. Too many of these Albion athletes just weren't at the races. But at least Gaffer was on song enough to shake hands with the Spartak skipper then win the toss. Carl, too, was fully able to place the ball on the centre-spot and – when the thankfully non-Greek ref whistled to start the match – roll a short pass sideways to Keats.

Keats, however, might just as well have had his shirt still over his head. The ball skidded under his boot and went straight to Titov, the oncoming Spartak midfielder.

That was the last sniff Albion got before going one-nil down.

Luke, who always lined up wide on the right for kick-offs, could only stare in disbelief. Titov – Russia's 1998 Player of the Year – nutmegged Narris, Half-Fat *and* Chrissie before slipping a gem of a through-ball inside Craig to Luis Robson who had steamed upfield as soon as the Russians won possession.

He reached the ball right on the edge of the Albion box. Gaffer was too far away to close him down. But somehow Cool F, who was even further over, managed to get across and cover for him. Sliding in with a trademark precision tackle from the side, he nicked the ball off Robson's toe and sent it trickling back safely towards Madman's Albion goal.

Safely. Now that word can mean different things in different circumstances. *Normally* a ball rolling gently back to a goalkeeper – with no opposition player making a challenge – is a completely safe thing. *Normally* that would have been the case with Madman. But this, tonight, was not a normal situation.

The Albion keeper just hadn't found his bearings yet. In his mind he was still being tossed around in the back of that Russian ex-army truck. And even before he coiled back his leg to hoof the ball upfield, Luke could see he was going to miss it. And oh, did he miss by a mile! Even the breeze he made was too distant to make the ball veer off course. So on it trundled, under his foot, over the line.

Russians one, Raw Prawns nil! The Spartak faithful went bananas. Just thirty seconds gone and their side was level on aggregate. Better still for them, in a sense they had taken the lead. For if no one else now scored all night, *their* team would go through on the away-goals-count-double rule. Every single Albion player, official and supporter (except Carl) realized that. And the shell-shocked looks on their silent faces said it all: this was a major disaster.

Straight from the restart, Spartak almost scored again. Five times in the next twenty minutes they should have added to their tally. Only some heroic last-ditch defending from Gaffer, Frederick, Luke (in a deeply-withdrawn role) and – surprisingly for a striker – Carl managed to keep the Russian marauders at bay.

Apart from those four, none of the Albion players could get a rhythm going. Which certainly wasn't true of Benny, Terry and Jimbo – who were dancing around like dervishes on the touchline in their attempts to buck up the team.

The Russians in the crowd could definitely smell blood. The way they roared on the men in red sent a chill up the back of Luke's neck. And now and then, when he paused for a breather, he scanned the seats and wondered how many Pineapple People were up there – watching, checking, gloating.

They must have felt well pleased with events so far. Already a goal to the good, and with Albion appearing to give a masterclass in How-To-Throw-A-Game. As far as they were concerned, Carl was really coming up trumps. But Carl, of course, knew nothing about any of this. And the funny thing was – he was playing a blinder.

The longer the half went on, the better he got. Not just working like a Trojan in defence, but holding up the ball expertly during Albion's rare surges forward – and peppering Filimonov's goal with a series of ambitious but intelligent long-shots. The best of these, just after the half-hour, actually beat the keeper but scraped past his far post. If the Pineapple People thought he'd *meant* to miss by such a whisker, they must have had a very high opinion of him indeed.

As half-time approached, the wind at last began to go out of Spartak's sails. Luke found he was getting more time on the ball. Frederick and Gaffer too, now under less pressure, had a bit of space to pass the ball out from the back instead of simply wellying it. And Carl made a couple of dazzling runs from halfway that were ended only by fine full-stretch stops from the keeper.

Over on the line, Benny and Co were slowing down. Like Luke, they must have hoped the storm had been weathered. All Albion had to do now was get to half-time without conceding again. That was all. It wasn't much to ask. Was it?

21

It happened in the third minute of time added on. No one knew *why* three minutes of injury time were played. As far as Luke remembered, no trainer had been on. The only injury had been to Albion's reputation as a serious football team. But now at last all the groggies were looking in much better shape.

Then Spartak got a lucky break in midfield. Half-Fat slightly mistimed a header and the ball went out of play instead of up to Keats. From the quickly taken throw, Titov and Baranov played a one-two around Craig. Titov hared on to the byline and slung in a low cross. He didn't take much trouble over it. He knew the whistle was about to go.

And the whistle did go. To signal Spartak's second strike of the night. For the ball cannoned against Narris' shins, pinged up on to the bar, cannoned down and – quite clearly to everyone – crossed the Albion goal line. *Phiz og.* Or auto-goal as they call it in Russia.

Albion's second of the evening. The ref blew for the goal, then blew again at once for half-time.

Spartak two Albion nil (agg. three-two). The Albion fans roared their protests at the ref all the way back to the tunnel. But none of the players tried to dispute the goal. The whole ball had crossed the line fair and square. Or fair and round. And refs never change their minds about goals anyway. And besides, the Albion lads needed to get themselves properly prepared for what now lay up ahead. Not the second half. But Benny's ballistic half-time rant.

He started it even before the first Albion player stepped off the grass. "Right! You, You, You, You, You, You and You!" he roared, stabbing an accusing finger at Madman, Craig, Dennis, Half-Fat, Narris, Chrissie and Keats. "You're all going *nowhere*! After a first-half display like that, you don't deserve even a *whiff* of half-time tea! Turn yourselves around and get back out there – I'm putting you through an extra trainin' session. Terry, Ruel – I need you too!"

And he meant it! The Sorry Seven all had to troop back out into the middle. Then Benny, Tel and Ruel immediately started putting them through their paces: press-ups, sit-ups, star-jumps... The crowd loved it – Rocky's lot and the Russian fans alike, especially after Princey and the other subs decided to get stuck in too –

while Gaffer, Luke, Frederick and Carl looked on wide-eyed.

"As skipper I suppose I really should be out there," sighed Gaffer. "Leading by example, you know? You lads enjoy your cuppa." And off he trotted to join in.

"Well, I'm parched," declared Carl, marching off down the tunnel. "I need my tea." Luke and Cool F turned to follow, just out of his earshot.

"This is a nightmare," Luke murmured to his mate. "It looks as if we're doing just what the Pineapple People wanted. Two-nil at half time. What if the score stays that way now? And the way we're playing tonight, it might."

Frederick shrugged. "We've just gotta score ourselves. Rewrite the script."

At that moment, Carl stepped into the dressing room where a puzzled-looking TAFKAG was waiting. "Hey, what's this?" Luke heard Carl ask.

As he and Frederick went inside themselves, they saw what Carl was talking about. There in the middle of the dressing-room floor was a great slatted wooden crate, the size of a small telephone box. "Weird city," frowned TAFKAG. "Doesn't look much like tea and biscuits to me. Maybe it's one of those *samovar* thingies – you know? – that the Russians brew up in."

"Or maybe it's the Dog," grinned Carl, "sent ahead in a parcel by Vealy?" But as he went closer to the mystery package, he started to sniff. TAFKAG did the same. "I'd recognize that smell anywhere," cried Carl. "It's pineapples!"

"*Pineapples?*" asked Luke, peering through the slats, and yes – that's exactly what was nestling fruitily inside. "There must be a hundred in there. And I thought there was meant to be a serious shortage over here."

"Somebody's been stockpiling," nodded Frederick. "And look – there's a note."

He tore off a single sheet pinned to the side. The writing on it was in English – a bit wobbly but completely readable. "*Thank you, Albion!*" it said. "*Half job now done. Here is next down payment. Look out of window for rest. Twenty-five thousand already! Same again at final whistle!*"

"What in the name of Simon and Garfunkel is *that* all about?" asked TAFKAG.

"D'you think it's a wind-up?" said Carl.

"I only wish it was," Luke muttered, crossing to the high, opened window with Frederick. They both had to stand on the bench to get a look outside. And there it stood: a rear view of another one of the Pineapple People's monster trucks, jampacked with at least a couple of hundred more crates. "'Twenty-five thousand'..." Luke said to himself.

"'Same again at final whistle'..." Frederick murmured back.

"That makes fifty thousand," Luke continued,

turning to face Cool F as the penny dropped. "If we go down two-nil, they're going to pay us with fifty thousand *pineapples*!"

"Pay?" asked Carl. "What for? And who are *they*?"

"And where's the half-time tea?" added TAFKAG, a little unhelpfully.

"Sit down, both of you," said Luke to both the men. "I think it's time that Frederick and I told you what's been going on ever since 7:30 this evening."

And then, as best they could, the two boys explained about one of the biggest misunderstandings in the history of international match-fixing.

22

It took Carl a while to grasp what he was being told. In fact the buzzer was sounding to call them back for the second half before he finally stammered:

"Oh *w-w-wow*! So they didn't just *give* me that one pineapple, then? It was all a part of some vile deal? But why didn't they *s-say*?"

"They did," Luke told him. "Just not clearly enough."

"Communication breakdown," Cool F nodded. They were all out in the tunnel by now and heading back towards the pitch. Carl was quite visibly trembling.

"But can't we just *tell* these Pineapple dudes the wires got crossed?" said TAFKAG.

"Somehow I don't think they'd be prepared to listen," Luke smiled grimly as they came out under the floodlights to find Benny finishing off his unscheduled training session. "Besides, we've got forty-five minutes of football to play."

"And that's *all* we've got to do," said Frederick

firmly. "Play football. We can do all our talking with our feet, yeah?"

"Spot on," agreed Luke. "They want us to lose two-nil. So we've just got to score ourselves. Once, twice – it doesn't matter. That way, we'll prove once and for all that we've got *no* interest in fixing the score."

"Y-yes," said Carl, as white as a Leeds shirt now, "but if we do score, the Pineapple People aren't going to be very pleased, are they? W-what d'you think they might do to us? I mean, they had *guns* and stuff out at that house. Atomic *weapons*..."

"Let's worry about that later," Luke suggested. "But in the meantime, Carl, the best thing *you* can do is stick an absolute belter in the net."

"For Albion!" TAFKAG added before heading off to his seat, clenching his fist and jutting out his unshaven chin. "For England! For Honesty!"

"'Nuff respect!" Cool F agreed, high-fiving both the other players. Then they ran off to take up their positions in the starting line-up for the second forty-five. Yet Carl, it had to be said, still didn't look a very happy goal-hunter.

Even so, the rest of the Albion team gave Rocky's Lot plenty to cheer when battle was resumed. Benny had clearly given the Sicko Seven a rattling good shakedown over the interval. Now all of them, from Madman to Keats, were looking the business. Spartak too seemed happy to sit back on their lead. So for most of the game's third quarter it was all one-way traffic – in Albion's favour.

Chrissie and Luke sent a stream of crosses deep into the Moscow box. And with Filimonov starting to flap, Keats had two great chances to nod Albion back into the contest. Both his headers, however, were cleared on the line. Soon after, a long-range raker from Narris hit the angle of post and crossbar.

But then came a quite bizarre sequence of goal-attempts – and they all fell to the same Albion player. First there was a one-on-one with the keeper, then a free near-post header, an unchallenged shot from the edge of the six-yard box, and, finally and most unmissably, a tap-in that even Jimbo might have put away. But every single chance went begging. To almost everyone's astonishment, the nerve-wracked Carl Davey made a complete and utter horlicks of them all.

His A-plus rating for the first half had sunk to Z-minus for the second. Luke had heard of players with two left feet but Carl now seemed to have a hundred of them. And Luke could see as clear as day what the problem was.

The Man with the Petrifying Passport Photo wasn't *trying* to foul up again and again (even if the Pineapple People in the crowd might have thought he was). Carl just couldn't get his brain into gear. His mind wasn't on the job in hand. All he could think about was the mess he'd get into if he scored – and the mess he *might* get into if he didn't. For if he scored, he would be letting down the Pineapple People. Yet if he didn't, he would be betraying the true spirit of football itself. It left him so knotted up, he couldn't perform the simplest feat with a football.

Luke saw all this. And from the looks he exchanged with Cool F, his mate saw it too. But as the minutes ticked away, and the score remained the same, just *knowing* what was wrong didn't put it right. And over on the Albion bench, another big problem was now rearing its corkscrew-haired, bespectacled head.

Jimbo was stripping off and getting ready to enter the fray! He'd told Benny that he intended to come on at some stage. This, apparently, was the moment.

Luke felt a sudden surge of anger. It was too much! First the Pineapple People sticking their stupid oar in. Now Jimbo Freakshow Prince about to scupper Albion's chances for good and all. This wasn't proper football. This wasn't the game that Luke had known and loved for so long. It had all got too complicated. And yet at bottom, as Benny was always saying, footie was such a beautifully *simple* thing.

So – narrowing his eyes, gritting his teeth,

and throwing back his shoulders – Luke decided that the time had come to remind everyone of that.

Breaking into a sudden infield run, he called for a layback from Keatso and got it. The ball came to him just inside the centre-circle, on Spartak's side of the halfway line. Keats then peeled away to make a great far-post run, taking two defenders with him, and opening up a clear sight of the goal for Luke.

Now there are clear sights and clear sights. You can sometimes, for instance, get a clear sight of the Great Wall of China from the moon. But that doesn't mean you can then hoof a football down and hope to hit it. There's the small matter of distance to take into account as well. And as far as the Spartak defence was concerned, Luke was *way* too far out to take a poke. Almost fifty yards in anybody's language. So no one rushed up to close him down.

Luke nudged the ball forward a yard or two, glanced at the posts and the keeper between them, and again he felt that sudden, electrifying surge of anger. Pineapple People! Player-chairmen! *Pah!* He felt himself swelling up, feeling as powerful as Popeye after fifty tins of spinach.

Simple! he told himself. That's how football ought to be. Here's the ball, there's the goal. Now here's my right foot kicking it, and there goes the ball in a high, swerving arc over everybody's heads – including the stranded keeper's. And down it drops, just under the bar and into the net for ... a goal. *Simple!*

And he wasn't wrong. It had looked simple enough for any kid in a park to have done it. But possibly only one kid in world football could have pulled it off. Luke Green, Albion's Studless Sensation, had just scored an away goal!

23

Two thousand English throats opened to salute one of the finest UEFA Cup strikes ever seen. Over on the Albion bench, the staff and subs went ape. Out on the pitch ten awestruck team-mates knelt before Luke in adoration – then jumped up and dragged him back down to earth in a riotous celebration.

But a deathly silence fell on anyone in the stadium who wasn't a Brit. And when the match restarted, that stunned silence grew deeper by the minute. Somehow it swamped even the happy chanting of Albion's faithful few.

Rocky and Co couldn't have been more pleased. Luke's fifteenth strike of the season had brought Albion level on aggregate with Spartak. If things stayed that way, there would be thirty minutes of extra time. Then if the deadlock *still* hadn't been broken – joy of joys: it would go to a penalty shoot-out! For in Madman Mort, Albion had just about the best spot-kick stopper in the business.

Most of the Albion players, too, really had their tails up. They weren't going to sit back now. Instead they bombed forward, down both flanks and through the centre, in search of a goal that would settle the tie within the regular ninety minutes. It was hard to think of these same men staggering around in a daze just an hour or so before. The way they were pinging the ball about, they already looked worthy UEFA Cup semi-finalists. (And a whole lot better than the twenty-third-best team in Nationwide Division Three. So maybe, just for once, that league table *was* telling a little white lie about their capabilities?)

But a handful of the hooped heroes weren't looking quite so hot as the rest. One of these was Keats. He'd given his best ever since half-time, and now he had very little left in the tank. He wasn't known as Eighty Minutes Aberdeen for nothing. And from the five fingers Benny was holding up, there must have been just five minutes of the ninety left. Keatsy was past his play-by date.

The second pooper in hoops was Mr Davey. He'd had a nightmare of a second half – and after the Albion goal, he might as well have really been asleep. He wandered about in a dream, the frown on his face so deep you could have heard an echo if you'd shouted into it. He could, of course, simply have been trying to work out the aggregate score. But Luke knew there was more to it.

He knew because he had the same thing on his own mind. And so, he could tell, did Cool F. Both boys knew as well as Carl that Albion's goal had *not* been in the Pineapple People's script. However much money they had staked on Spartak winning two-nil, they could kiss it all goodbye now. Luke had upset their grubby little pineapplecart and no mistake. They would not be best pleased. But as Carl had asked before, how would they show their displeasure?

Even as they honed in on the Spartak goal, Luke and Frederick kept glancing into the crowd. What were they looking for? Mafia men with poisoned blow-darts at their lips? Telescopic rifle sights? Bazookas? Cruise-missile launchpads?

If so, they spotted none of these.

But there *was* some crowd movement in the stand behind the dug-outs, the stand behind which that vast fruit truck had been parked. Luke craned his neck to try to see what was going on. His eyes popped.

Then he stopped pretending to play and peered harder. Pairs of Pineapple People guys in furry hats and long coats were streaming in from outside, and they were lugging great ... crates. As far as Luke could see, they were heading fast for the front rows now – brushing stewards aside as they went – and tearing the crates open.

He swapped glances with Frederick, who had also taken a brief time-out from the game. But Cool F's gaze had been lower than Luke's. He hadn't been watching the PP goons arriving. He'd seen something just as gobsmacking around the Albion bench. And when he pointed it out, Luke saw too.

There, just beyond the touchline, stood six guys in a row: two UEFA officials, two men in Albion tracksuit tops, two players in blue and white hoops. The officials were holding up substitute boards – informing Carl Davey and Keats Aberdeen that their time was up and would they come in, please? The first tracksuit top belonged to Terry V, who was giving last-minute instructions to the two waiting subs. The second was being worn by – could it be? *Could* it? Oh yes it could! A lanky guy with gelled-up hair, Raybans and a pair of green Lurex cycling shorts underneath. None other than Neil Veal: players' agent!

"Hah!" cried Luke in disbelief. For there alongside him, under a shaggy mane of hair that looked like a little black sheep itself, stood the long-lost Shepherd in Shooting Boots, the King of Keepy-Uppy, the terrier who was terrified of transport: Big Dog Mez!

**"Woof! Woof!! Woof!!! Woof!!!!
WOOF!!!!! WOOF!!!!!! WOOF!!!!!!!"**

roared the Albion fans in ecstasy as soon as
they spotted him (whilst ignoring the other
Albion sub at his side, Joker Jimbo Prince). It
was *so* long since they'd been able to drool
over Dogan's silken skills and his paranormal
pace. They were almost as thrilled as Neil Veal
himself, who now wouldn't have to suffer death
by vodka.

But first Dog had to get on to the pitch. And
when Spartak's Khlestov cleared the ball into
touch by the dug-outs, the ref whistled and
waved for the changeover. What happened next
should have been straightforward. It wasn't.

Clapped-out Keats saw the board and began
to drag himself over to the bench. Carl wouldn't
have seen it if it had whizzed across the pitch
and bitten him on the bottom. So Luke and
Frederick had to take an arm each and escort
him off. But when they were still a few yards
short of the touchline, Carl started to struggle
and back away, with a look of total panic in his
eyes.

Luke had been concentrating on Carl. Now he
looked up into the crowd.

Uh-oh.

24

All the Pineapple People were starting to bombard the touchline.

Not with toilet rolls – like in England. Not with ticker-tape – like in Argentina. Not with firecrackers – like in Spain. No, here in chilly Moscow they did things differently. The men in furry hats were showing their utter disgust at Albion's goal with a hard rain of big juicy pineapples!

Lots and lots and *lots* of pineapples. Dozens of them. Scores. Hundreds. It could even have been thousands! Carl's reward. The payment he was not now going to get – and which he had never remotely wanted in the first place.

But these fruits were like gold dust in Russia just now. So there were plenty of punters in the crowd who *did* want them. Almost as soon as each pineapple hit the ground, a fan leapt out of his or her seat to snaffle it up.

As a result, for a short while, chaos reigned. It wasn't immediately helped by the soldiers in front of the Albion fans rushing across the pitch to restore order, because half of *them* were more interested in pocketing a pineapple before dealing out a bit of discipline.

Both astonished sets of players retreated to the centre-circle – Carl still among them. Meanwhile the ref was deep in conversation with his assistants. Clearly he was wondering if he should take the teams off. Or even abandon the game. Maybe, in a way, that was what the spoilsport Pineapple People had been hoping for.

But soon the soldiers took control – driving everyone back into their seats, forcing the Pineapple Marksmen right out of the stand, and restoring some much-needed order. Luckily, not a single person had been hit in the pineapple shower. Not yet, anyway. For it still wasn't quite done and dusted.

Luke, who with Frederick was now leading Carl back to the bench, saw it all. If he hadn't seen it with his own eyes, he wouldn't have believed it. But there it was. As plain as day. At least to Luke (and, thankfully – as it turned out later – not to very many others).

As the ref waved again for the substitutions to be made, Dogan raced on to the turf to a tumultuous welcome from the away fans:

"How MUCH is that Doggy on the pitch there? We DO hope that Dog's not for sale!"

The Dog, power-thighs pumping like pistons, waved and mouthed "Yo!" to his Posse (in the form of: "I am exceedingly pleased to meet you!").

Meanwhile Jimbo was prancing up and down on the touchline, waiting to high-five Carl as he came off, then take his place on the pitch. Luke could almost hear the heads of the other Albion players drop behind him. True, Carl was having a five-star stinker. But that still smelled pretty sweet alongside even the best that Jimbo could offer. And although Carl had missed some sitters, he hadn't given any crazy goals *away* – which was Jimbo's very own speciality.

Oh *why* did the useless player-chairman have to choose this moment to make his comeback? Why couldn't he wait till Macclesfield on Saturday? Albion still had it all to play for. But Jimbo would foul things up as sure as eggs were eggs. Luke knew that every Albionite in Moscow had just one wish: *Oh please, please keep Princey off the park!* But only one man had the courage, the vision and the talent to make that wish come true. That man was Terry Vaudeville.

He saw his chance with five pineapples that still lay just inside the touchline. As Luke, Carl and Cool F approached, Terry V darted forward and scooped up a couple. Then, half-turning, he lobbed them up high into the grateful crowd.

The fans at once cried out noisily for more. Terry obliged. He scooped, half-turned, and threw the next two – a bit harder and a bit lower down.

That left one. And this one had a name on it. "Pozhaluysta! Pozhaluysta! Pozhaluysta!" bayed the out-reaching Russians. *Please! Please! Please!* Terry scooped a third time. As he did so, Luke definitely saw him glance backwards to check where Jimbo was standing. *Definitely.* There was no question about it. And right away, he swung around like a baseball pitcher and he flung that last pineapple with awesome force right into the chest of the player-chairman!

"Sorry, oh sorry, sorry, *sorry!*" Terry yelled as Jimbo was propelled backwards almost into Row F. Then he rushed up to apologize in person for the "accident". But even as he did so, he tugged on the sleeve of the official holding up the board with Carl's number on it and shook his head: no more substitutions.

Benny shot up off the bench. "Stay on, Carl!" he roared, picking up the pineapple that had done all the necessary damage. "Jimbo's in no fit state to come on now! Just get stuck in out there! Like you did in the first half!"

Luke, spellbound by Terry's ingenuity, let Carl go. So did Cool F. The ref whistled for play to begin again, with a throw-in to the Albion just over halfway. But Carl was still *well* out of it. He wandered like a sleepwalker towards Benny, who waved and bellowed at him, "Back! Back! I want you out there!"

But still Carl was way off-message. And when he crossed the touchline, Benny had to grab hold of him and physically turn him right round. "Get back on that *pitch*!" he commanded. "What's *wrong* with you?! Get your *skates* on!"

And then Benny pulled off his tactical masterstroke. As Craig took the throw straight to Dog – to give him a nice early touch – Carl began to dawdle back over the touchline. Which wasn't good enough for Benny. Dopey Davey needed a proper wake-up call – and Benny had just the right prop to hand. Coiling back his arm in the way that Craig Edwards did before every game, he let fly with the pineapple for a smasher of a hit on Carl's right buttock.

"Aaaarrrrrrrggggggggghhhhhhhhhhhh!" screamed Carl, letting out all his pent-up emotion from the last dreadful forty-odd minutes. Suddenly his worries fell away as he fizzed off in the direction of the Spartak goal. All that mattered was football. Nothing else. Nothing *ever*.

Luke had rarely seen him move so fast. He was like a balloon that Benny had blown up but forgotten to knot. Making the same sort of noise as well, as he rocketed past and on towards the edge of Filimonov's box. Meanwhile, back near halfway, Dogan's first three Euro-touches in three months had been real corkers.

Taking Craig's throw on the first bounce, he spun away from Parfyonov and left him for dead. Baranov steamed in but SuperDog simply nudged the ball to his left then ran around his right to collect it. The nervy Spartak defence all expected him to race on and try his luck against the next six players in his way.

But Dogan Mezir was no Darren Huckerby. He knew that there was more to top-flight football than dribbling on and on until somebody knocked you over. Carl's turbo-run towards the near post had caught his eye. And with no backlift at all, the Dog nestled his boot beneath the ball and dinked up a luscious thirty-yard pass right into Carl's path.

There wasn't a chance in a million that any red shirt could turn in time to keep pace with Dynamite Davey. Before the ball began to drop, it was a two-horse race between Carl and keeper Filimonov. And even that looked like a hopeless mismatch. Carl was covering so much ground, he was outstripping the *ball* as well as every opponent. Which wasn't, to the watching Luke, good news.

For Dog's pass had been perfect for any normal person to run on to and smack on the volley at the goal. But now the ball was dropping down *behind* Carl.

And Carl didn't seem to notice. He just kept barrelling on – putting the fear of God into Filimonov, who was bravely rushing out, but now seemed about to be steamrollered. For a vital split-second the goalie held back. And in that same blinking of an eye Carl checked too. Not just to avoid hitting the guy in green, but also to tilt his upper body forward and kick up both legs behind him until he was almost horizontal. Then, just as the ball came within kicking distance, he flicked up both heels – scorpion-style – made the sweetest of connections, and sent it over his own head, then Filimonov's, *and into the gaping net!*

The net wasn't all that was gaping. If anyone in the stadium had been able to say two words, they would have been "Rene Higuita". Or quite possibly that same player's nickname: "El Loco". For the famous old Colombian goalie had patented the scorpion kick years before. But he had only ever used it to save goals, not to score them.

And what a goal this was to score. This made it Spartak two, Albion two on the night – and four-three to Ash Acre's Aces across the two legs – although Carl himself was probably the last person in Moscow to be sure about that. Not that he cared. With a little help from ten friends in blue hoops, he was too busy celebrating the greatest goal of his career. The goal that would take Albion through to the UEFA Cup's last four. The goal that proved beyond doubt – to anyone who cared to watch – that *no* amount of pineapples could tempt him to throw a game.

"One Carly Davey!"
bayed the pilgrims from Ash Acre reviving an age-old chant,

**"There's Only One Carly Davey!
One Carly DAVEY – And His Hair's Very Wavy!"**

Benny was up off the bench punching great holes in the Moscow night sky. Keats had found a last drop of energy to dance a little jig. Even Terry, who had the semi-conscious Jimbo flopped over one arm like a rag doll, was waving his magic sponge and hollering, "You Beauty, Carl! You Great Ugly *Beauty*!" And Luke could only grin when he remembered what he had said to Carl at the interval: *The best thing you can do is stick an absolute belter in the net!*

But it wasn't over yet. Not quite. There were still three more minutes to kill off. Yet, after Carl's sudden injection of pace, *everything* seemed quicker – even the passage of time. And before Luke could say "This has been a thoroughly professional performance tonight from the Albion," the ref was giving it three sharp blasts and Spartak Moscow were UEFA Cup history for another season.

Benny leapt jubilantly out on to the pitch, closely followed by Terry and the moany-groany Jimbo. Behind them, the soldiers all formed up in a line to face the main stand, daring anyone to start another pineapple avalanche. There was going to be *no* more trouble in the Lokomotiv Stadium that night. Carl and the Albion lads were out of the Pineapple People's reach for now. All bets were off. And within ninety minutes they would be winging their way safely back to Britain (apart from Dog and Vealy, of course, who had a date with a tandem).

They dashed across to where their loyal fans were having a mass victory hug, jumped over the wall and joined in too. The last Luke saw of Benny, he was being tossed high in the air by about a hundred arms – and performing the worst-ever scorpion kick in the history of goal reconstructions.

Narris, Half-Fat and Madman were bobbing and bellowing on the blue-and-white ocean, looking as if they'd already drunk several times their own body-weights in post-match Russian champagne. Dog sat astride a plastic inflatable tandem with ITV's Jim Rosenthal who was trying to interview him from behind, while Chrissie gleefully zonked Dennis and Craig on their heads with a massive rubber pineapple. Even the very grown-up Gaffer was giving Neil Veal, of all people, an especially firm handshake.

"You showed 'em, lads!" cried TAFKAG, emerging from the heaving, chanting and (to be quite honest) stinking multitude to give first Luke then Frederick a big sloppy kiss. "Oh man, this is a right-on victory for the true values of football. *No one* can say the Albion are match-fixers, right? Oh yeah, baby, *yeah*!"

Luke and Frederick grinned at each other. It had been a close-run thing, but they'd just about managed it – thanks to a marvellous bit of magic from the guy who now popped out of the pack right between them: Wavy-Haired Carl Davey.

"D'you think we're gonna be OK now, lads?" Carl asked, pulling their heads in towards him. "I mean, we've upset those Pineapple People pretty badly, right?"

"Yeah," laughed Luke, pointing at the soldiers, "but we've got the army to protect us now! Not to mention Benny's *Barmy* Army here!"

"Nuff said," agreed Cool F. "But maybe, just to be on safe side till we're out of Russia, you could – uh – disguise yourself a bit, Carl?"

Frederick raised an eyebrow at Luke as some of the other players gathered round. They looked in puzzlement from Cool F to Carl to Luke. For they, of course, were still completely in the dark about the monstrous mix-up with the Pineapple People.

"Disguise?" asked Carl. "Really? How? What do you suggest?"

Luke smiled. He saw what Frederick was getting at. "Well," he said mischievously, "you looked pretty good in that passport photo of yours. Why don't you make yourself look like *that* again – just till we've left the country?"

"Oh, Noooooooooooooooo!" yodelled the other players, and a fair few of the fans as well. "Never! Please, not THAT!"

Then they all grabbed hold of soccer's new Mr Scorpion and threw him so high in the air that he almost needed oxygen before he came back down!

Creatures

The Series With Bite!

Everyone loves animals. The birds in the trees. The dogs running in the park. That cute little kitten.

But don't get too close. Not until you're sure. Are they ordinary animals – or are they creatures?

1. Once I Caught a Fish Alive
Paul's special new fish is causing problems. He wants to get rid of it, but the fish has other ideas...

2. If You Go Down to the Woods
Alex is having serious problems with the school play costumes. Did that fur coat just move?

3. See How They Run
Jon's next-door neighbour is very weird. In fact, Jon isn't sure that Frankie is completely human...

4. Who's Been Sitting in My Chair?
Rhoda's cat Opal seems to be terrified ... of a chair! But then this chair belongs to a very strange cat...

Look out for these new creatures...

5. Atishoo! Atishoo! All Fall Down!
Chocky the mynah bird is a great school pet. But now he's turning nasty. And you'd better do what he says...

6. Give a Dog a Bone
A statue of a faithful dog sounds really cute. But this dog is faithful unto death. And beyond...

Creatures – you have been warned!

Paul Stewart

Football Mad
2-1 up in the inter-school cup final, captain
Gary Connell finds the net … at the wrong end!
Now cup glory rests on a tricky replay…

Football Mad 2
Offside!
The inter-school cup is up for grabs again. But
Craig won't be playing. He's been dropped –
and he's not happy…

Football Mad 3
Hat-trick!
Could it be cup-final number three?
Goalkeeper Danny is in trouble. New team
coach Mr Carlton has really got it in for him…

HURRICANE HAMISH
Mark Jefferson

HURRICANE HAMISH
THE CALYPSO CRICKETER

Hurricane Hamish has always been a bit special –
ever since he was found washed up on a Caribbean
beach wrapped in an MCC towel. He's only twelve,
but he can bowl fast. Really fast. So fast he might
be about to play for the West Indies...

HURRICANE HAMISH
THE CRICKET WORLD CUP

Hurricane Hamish is back – and now he's in
England, determined to help the West Indies win the
Cricket World Cup. But England is so cold! The
grounds are so wet and slippery that Hurricane
can't even stay standing, let along bowl fast...

*"The ideal literary companion for this summer's
Carnival of Cricket – the World Cup."*
Lord MacLaurin, Chairman of the England and
Wales Cricket Board

*"Mark Jefferson has scored a real winner with
Hurricane Hamish ... this pacey romp of a book."*
Christina Hardyment, The Independent

"A novel which, like its hero, has pace and heart."
Nicolette Jones, The Sunday Times